MISS YOU WHEN YOU'RE GONE

E.G. STONE

TARNEY BRAE CREATIVE ENDEAVOURS

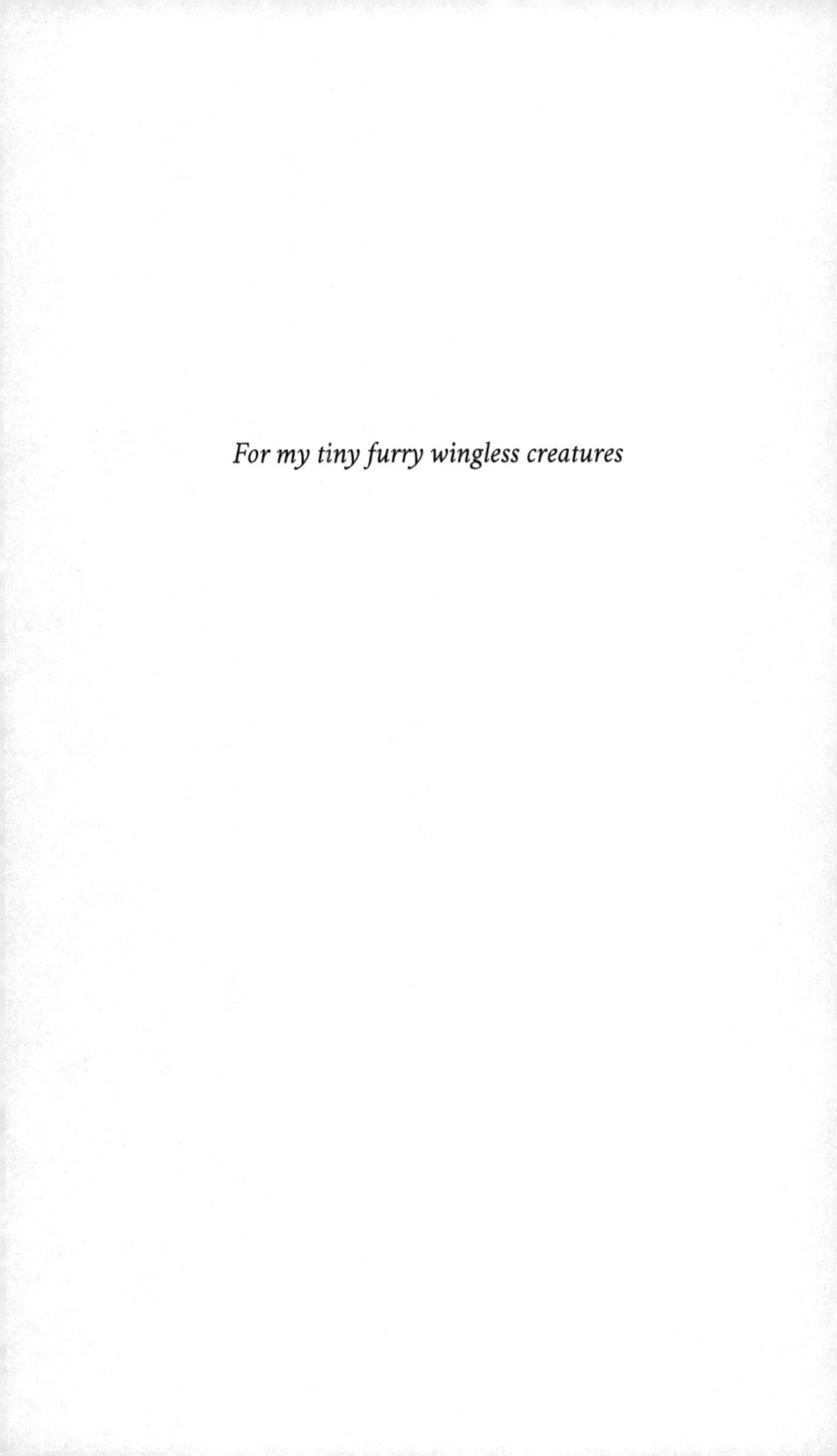

For my tiny furry wingless creatures

CONTENTS

"I'm going to die," I groaned, face half-buried in the cushions of my couch, my blanket pulled up to my chin, a pile of tissues collecting in the rubbish bin next to the coffee table. My coffee, which I'd had Yolanda prepare about half-an-hour ago, was untouched. It was tragic and I felt horrible.

"You can't die, Cal," Agravane said, sounding ridiculously cheerful. He sat in an overstuffed armchair at a ninety-degree angle to the couch, laptop in hand, only looking at the muted action movie on the television across from the couch every thirty seconds or so. Considering he was technically keeping me company while I died a horrible, slow death rather than working in my marketing office a floor below us, I wasn't going to complain about his being distracted from work.

"It's been three days," I grumbled. "Just kill me now so I can get over it."

"Would that even work?" Agravane mused, tilting his head. I was about to suggest that we could give it a shot—surely it couldn't be worse than my current state —when Agravane burst out laughing, pointing at me. "Your face! You looked so hopeful! You can't *honestly* think killing you would get rid of your cold?"

"It's got rid of a bunch of other problems." I reached for another tissue and honked into the stupid piece of flimsy paper, my nose throbbing.

"It's a cold, Cal, you're not dying." Agravane looked smugly at me.

"Yeah, well, until your stupid magical butt can actually *catch* a cold, don't tell me I'm not dying." My head ached, my mouth was cracked and dry, my nose was an everrunning faucet and I felt like I had a ball of phlegm stuck in my lungs.

"One of the perks of having a magical butt," Agravane retorted. I considered throwing my used tissue at him, but that would have required movement, so I just grunted horribly and buried my head in my blanket.

I used to think that being accidentally immortal as a result of working for Death as his marketing agent, while also in possession of Reaper abilities named Sebastian, having no soul, and various other sundry things that came with living full time in the magical realm of Elsewhere, that I surely couldn't get sick. I hadn't got sick since being hired by Death, unless you count being not-quite-killed numerous times. Turns out, I was just as susceptible to colds now as I had been while living in the mortal realms as nothing more than a slightly ignorant human.

I hated the world.

The afternoon progressed in a fairly sedate manner,

which is to say, I tried to breathe while Agravane did his work in relative silence, though I had the feeling he was probably playing games rather than doing marketing work. The occasional whoop of victory was a pretty good indication. Yolanda stopped in every now and then with updates on the office—my email was suspiciously quiet and the phone hadn't rung once, apparently—and to bring me tea or water or coffee or soup.

Then, just as the afternoon moved into evening and Agravane prepared to go home, Death strode into my apartment, the door slamming open behind him and his expression stormy.

"Your mother is a far more capable negotiator than I anticipated," Death grumbled. I did my best to hide a grin while I sniffled.

Last month, I had been sent back home to London to deal with a situation that my cousin Baz had caused, and in the process, Death had offered Baz a job as Justice. My cousin had then done the only intelligent thing he could and appointed my mother temporary power of attorney so she could negotiate terms and benefits on his behalf.

Death was a power of the universe, equal only to Life. He had skin the colour of a black hole, eyes that held the voids of the deep and was remarkably level-headed and reasonable. Life, his chaotic wife, was ever-changing and tempestuous, in both looks and personality. Neither one of them could stand up to my mother, Teresa Thorpe, and hope to come out unscathed. My mother was simply that capable.

For example: I was currently in possession of the former Justice's lifeforce, due to rather complicated circumstances. That meant Baz couldn't become Justice until I had given him my lifeforce. My mother had deemed this unacceptable and both Baz and I were able to keep our own lifeforces, negotiated by means of giving Baz holidays off. I have no idea how this happened, but it was also about the time that Life walked out of negotiations permanently.

"What happened this time?" I asked, my cold making me sound miserable instead of smug.

Death sank into the other armchair with a scowl, slumping until his shoulders were up to his ears and his chin touched his chest. His suit was as immaculate as ever, a charcoal grey with minuscule pinstripes, his waistcoat a deep shade of plum. It was the only part of him that looked unruffled.

"Sunglasses," Death said, as though this was the end of the world.

"Sunglasses?" Agravane frowned. "What's wrong with sunglasses? I mean, yes, we don't get much sun here in your lands, but the rest of Elsewhere and the mortal realms are relatively sunny."

Death shook his head. "She refused to blind Baz—"

"What?" I nearly sat up in shock, then collapsed back onto my pillow when my sinuses protested the change in elevation. I sniffled. "Baz does not need to be blind!"

In fact, I had a suspicion that a blind Baz would be infinitely more destructive than a sighted one. He was simply that chaotic. Even Life had once commented on it.

"Justice is blind," Death said. Right. As if that made it better. "But your mother was similarly offended, so we negotiated down to sunglasses. Dark sunglasses."

Baz was going to love that.

"In exchange for…?"

Death shook his head. "There was no exchange. Only adamant refusal. If I did not agree, the negotiations would be over."

Like I said, my mother was not cowed at all by Death, no matter that he could literally kill her with a touch. Life, who could actually do more significant damage, was so unnerved by my mother that she refused to interfere in the negotiations at all, despite the fact that Baz would technically work for both of them.

I was going to make some comment with high amounts of snark to Death, but coughed instead. Almost immediately, Yolanda appeared as if from nowhere, a steaming mug of broth in her hands. With surprising delicacy for a rock troll with the physique of a rugby player, Yolanda set the mug on the coffee table.

"Are you sick?" Death asked, tilting his head at me.

"Yes," I wheezed.

"Huh."

"Huh?" I sniffled and took a sip of the broth. It was too warm, but soothed my sore throat anyways. "Is that all you have to say?"

Death shrugged. "Just wondering who you caught it

from is all. There aren't many who can carry such a virus here in Elsewhere."

For all I knew, Life gave it to me just because she was bored. I decided not to answer Death.

As if I had conjured her from my thoughts, Life swanned through the door. She strutted into my apartment as though she owned the place, no concern for knocking or asking permission to enter. She gave a dismissive glance to her husband, then looked at me and nodded. "I need you to do a job for me," she said without preamble.

I coughed. "No."

Life quirked an eyebrow. "No? Need I remind you of our arrangement? You work for me, even if your job title is gofer."

"I work for you on a part-time basis, and I can't do anything right now," I said through gritted teeth. "I'm sick."

I think my answer must have startled her, because Life actually looked at me. She took in my prone form, the pillows, the blanket, the numerous beverages and pile of tissues in the rubbish bin. Her mouth formed a perfect 'O' and she tilted her head, as if I were an abstract painting where she expected sculpture, or something equally bizarre.

"Well, *that* won't do me any good. You'll have to get better."

"Yes, because I do this for my own pleasure." I pulled the blanket tighter around me. Death tried to suppress a chuckle. Agravane and Yolanda wisely stayed out of the argument, looking intently at Agravane's computer, as if he hadn't turned it off five minutes ago.

Life tossed her hair, and I'm sure had my sinuses been clear, I would have smelled her intoxicating scent. As it was, I just glared. Before I could do so much as sniffle, Life sauntered over to me, leaned over, and pressed her lips to my forehead.

Now, that might sound romantic, but people aren't supposed to actually touch Life. She was too powerful, too overwhelming. Had I been a normal human, a simple brush of her skin against mine would have sent so much life experience coursing through me that I would have burned up from the inside out and never been seen again. I was not a normal human and therefore could not die, but that didn't mean I felt none of the power of Life's kiss.

Generally, it was something I preferred to avoid, as it was extremely painful.

Like really, really painful.

My throat was too raw to scream. My limbs locked up, muscles tightening. I felt like I had just run several marathons simultaneously while also jumping off a cliff, falling in love, experiencing the worst grief I could imagine, and getting shot. Multiple times. My skin felt feverish, I'm pretty sure my hair was standing on end and I very nearly bit my tongue. And those were just the sensations I had words to describe.

A few seconds later and Life pulled back, smirking. My vision flared white for a moment. I blinked rapidly until everything looked normal, then pressed a hand to my head. I was almost certain I would find the impression of Life's lips permanently burned into my skin, but thankfully, there was nothing there. I straightened my glasses, sat up, and realised I could breathe normally.

Life had killed me.

She had also cured my cold.

I glared.

"That was unnecessarily dramatic," Death said. "You could have just willed him better."

Life waved a dismissive hand. "Don't be so boring. What fun would that have been?"

"Plenty," I said flatly. I was wearing my pyjama pants and a t-shirt I had stolen from Baz with the Tiny Dinosaurs With Phasers band logo. They were some obscure punk band that Baz enjoyed thoroughly, and while their music was…questionable at best, they did make a very comfortable shirt. It was not what I would have preferred to face Life in; with her, I liked to be girded in my best suits, my most impressive shoes and an expression that could ice over the desert. Instead, I crossed my arms and narrowed my eyes.

"You're no fun, did you know that?" Life huffed.

"I have been informed." I pushed my glasses up my nose. "What job did you need me to do?"

Life thrust out her hand and waved an embossed envelope in my face. I took it gingerly, half-expecting it to burst into flames, then opened it.

"This is an invitation for a coronation ceremony," I read, looking at the neat card inside, also embossed with what I suspected was real gold. "For the…Great Northern Ridge tribe of the—"

"No," Yolanda said, though I think it might have been a shout.

I turned to gape at her. Yolanda was a perpetually cheerful individual, with nothing but good things to say about the world unless she was around someone powerful who could notice her existence. She was not the sort to interrupt. Life terrified Yolanda, and I had never heard her do something so dramatic as shout in Life's presence.

"Um...?" I asked. "Is there something wrong?"

"No," Life said. "I just don't want to go. I have a marvellous week planned in the tropics and would have to postpone if I attended this coronation. So you're going in my place. Isn't that fun?"

"No," Yolanda said again, more seriously. Life scoffed and rolled her eyes.

"Just because they threw you off a cliff doesn't mean that Cal can't go in my place. Besides, rock trolls throw decent parties, especially when swearing in new rulers. And now that Cal is feeling better, he doesn't have any excuse. Ta ta!" Life turned on her heel and vanished before I could get a word in edge wise and ask any questions. She didn't even have the courtesy to close the door behind her, not that I was really surprised by that.

I looked to Death for some sort of answers, but he stood abruptly, straightened his necktie and left without a backwards glance, muttering about sunglasses. He closed the door to my apartment with a decisive click and I was left alone with Agravane and

Yolanda and an invitation in my hands that I was not certain I wanted to accept.

Agravane closed his computer and set it aside, giving Yolanda a pat on her hand, resting on the chair behind him. "It's going to be okay."

"What's going on here?" I asked, though I had a sinking feeling that I knew most of the answer.

See, Death hired capable people to work for him, but he could only hire them in the Instant of Death, the moment when we crossed into his realm, even if we could potentially be brought back through medical or magical means. Yolanda told me when I was first hired that she had started working for Death after her people rejected her. They were about to throw her out. I just hadn't realised she meant that literally.

"So the Great Northern Ridge tribe…" I prompted, answering part of my question for her. "They're your people?"

Yolanda winced. She shuffled over to the chair Death had vacated and threw herself into its embrace. Her massive form made the wooden frame creak ominously and she didn't really fit properly. Yolanda scrunched her knees up to her chest, making the chair look smaller.

She picked at the leather with her grey-green fingers. Nodded. "Yes, they're my people."

"And they threw you off a cliff?" Agravane asked, voice dripping with incredulity. Yolanda winced, but nodded.

"Yes, they threw me off a cliff," she said.

"That *sucks*." I tossed the invitation to the coffee table. "I'm sorry."

"Thank you." Yolanda gave a watery smile, but at least she was showing at least some of her usual cheer. Even if it was forced. We sat there in awkward silence for a few minutes, Agravane fiddling with his phone and Yolanda literally twiddling her thumbs. I wanted to ask more, wanted to know why her people had thrown her off a cliff, wanted to know why she was so opposed to this coronation celebration. Anything I asked would be intruding, though, and I didn't want to do that. I stared at the mug on the coffee table instead, mentally calculating the distance from the couch to the microwave.

"Fine!" Yolanda threw up her hands in the first fit of temper I had seen from her. Well, excepting that one time I got captured by vampires and she rescued me with her battle magic. I don't think that counts. "I'll tell you."

"We didn't ask," Agravane said, hand over his heart, eyes wide.

"You were thinking very loudly." Yolanda scowled, and it was so unlike her usual smile that I wanted to hug her. The emotion surged up through me to the point where I was out of my seat and wrapping my arms around her before I could even contemplate the emotion. My arms wouldn't meet all the way around her shoulders and I think both of us felt awkward after only a second. Yolanda patted my arm.

"Sorry," I said. "It just sort of seemed like a good idea."

"That's alright, Cal," Yolanda said. She patted my arm again. "You can let go, now."

I released her and shuffled back to my seat. Sebastian, the semi-sentient Reaper abilities I had, woke up for the first time in weeks and fixed me with a confused look. I shrugged mentally and it went back to sleep.

"You don't have to tell us if you don't want to," I said, trying to sound polite and concerned rather than monotonous. Some emotions were still difficult for me, even though it had been a decently long time since I had lost my soul. The theory that practice and time would make my soulless state more normal was definitely false. Most of the time, I felt nothing at all. The rest of the time, my emotions swung wildly from passion to despair, covering everything in between. To cover up this lack, I started talking rapidly. "I mean, I really would like to know, since it's both a terrible thing and also I have to go attend this party on Life's behalf, now that she killed me to cure my cold and—"

"Cal," Agravane said, interrupting me with a glare. "Drink your coffee and shut up."

My coffee was cold, but I did as he told me. Immediately, my body relaxed and reality stabilised around me to the point where I could think, even if it wasn't coherent.

"Rock trolls are not cave trolls," Yolanda started. "We have similar genetic structures, but they have a ruling system based on trial by combat. Rock trolls have a hairy…herey…hairadairy system."

I blinked. "Do you mean hereditary?"

Yolanda nodded.

Her English had improved by leaps and bounds since I started working with her, but correspondence courses only taught so much. She still had some of the strangest gaps in her vocabulary.

"How do you know genetic structures but not hereditary?" Agravane asked. I threw a pillow at him.

"My bloodline had been the ruling line of my tribe for generations," Yolanda continued as if Agravane hadn't spoken. "My father is—was—the current leader and as his only full-blood offspring, I was to assume power after his death. From a young age, I was taught the ways of our people on the understanding that I would rule. Only..." She trailed off and blushed, the skin around her nose and cheeks turning a burnt orange.

"Only?" I prompted.

"Only I..." Yolanda buried her face in her massive hands and mumbled out some words that I barely understood, let alone comprehended.

Agravane dropped his phone to the floor with a clatter, jaw dropping. "Wait, *what*?"

"What?" I asked. "What?!"

"She just said that she and a mountain nymph fell in love and declared themselves mates!" Agravane spluttered.

I blinked. Waited. Tried to sip at my still cold coffee in the hopes that it would somehow have got warmer in the last minute. Looked up. "Yeah, no, I don't understand what that means."

Yolanda chuckled, wiping her eyes from tears that

were definitely not from laughing. "You are a good person, Cal," she said.

I bobbed my head in a nod. "If you say so. But I still don't get it."

"Mountain nymphs are an offshoot of forest nymphs that split from the main line aeons ago," Agravane explained as if he were giving me a history lesson that everyone knew. "They're as beautiful and graceful as their forest cousins, only with an affinity for mountains. For a nymph to fall in love with a rock troll is like, well—"

"Like what?" I narrowed my eyes at Agravane and even Sebastian sat up to take notice. Was the aurai suggesting that Yolanda and this nymph couldn't be mates because the nymph was beautiful and Yolanda had massive muscles, stout figure and grey-green skin? I knew that the people of Elsewhere had some strange notions compared to the mortal world, but that seemed a little much, even for me.

"Like a unicorn and a dragon trying to produce offspring!" Agravane said, throwing his hands up. "It's physically impossible!"

Yolanda's shoulders were up by her ears and her fingers were digging into the arms of my chair as though it were the only thing holding her up. She was blushing furiously and her eyes were downcast.

I frowned, Sebastian doing the same from deep within me. Both of us focused our annoyance at Agravane until the air elemental shrank back.

"What?" he said. "Their species are genetically incompatible, that's just a fact. If she wanted to continue her family's bloodline, then that would have been a problem. Royal families *always* want to continue the bloodline. That's Elsewhere 101, Cal."

I wasn't going to argue genetics with the aurai. I just grabbed the invitation off the coffee table and waved it in front of Yolanda. "I have an idea."

"What?" she asked, misery lacing that simple word until it threatened to actually rain right in my living room.

"We're *both* going to that coronation party," I said firmly. "And we're going to parade in front of your people, showing them how freaking awesome you are until they either fall on their faces in apology or they admit defeat and are banished to a far off land."

I didn't know if I could annoy an entire tribe enough for them to consider banishment, but I would certainly try if it made Yolanda feel better. She blinked back some more tears.

"You don't have to do that, Cal," she murmured.

"Yes, I do. You're the best assistant I've ever had and I don't think I could ever function properly without you. Also, I need your help to pronounce your people's names right."

"At least it's not dwarfish," Agravane muttered. I jabbed my finger in his direction.

"Shut up, I'm still mad at you."

"Don't be mad at him, Cal," Yolanda said. "He was just stating a fact. We could never have properly had children, a lineage, Boulder and I. It's just...we didn't care. We thought our feelings were more important than some familial duty."

"I didn't mean to offend you," Agravane said, sounding at least sincere in his apology. "It was just startling is all. I of all people know about walking away from familial duty."

He had a point; I had helped rescue him from the Order of Silence, a group of assassins made up primarily of aurai. It was supposedly some great honour to one's family to join, but training also involved literally walking the line between Life and Death and was pretty much torture. No wonder he'd left.

"So, are we going to do this?" I asked, waving the invitation around again. "Because I have to go anyways, per my agreement with Life, and I'd really rather make this interesting."

Yolanda stared at the piece of paper like it could either save her or kill her, yellow eyes wide. She swallowed once, closed her eyes, then nodded. "Okay," she said.

I grinned, a fierce feeling flooding through me. I think Sebastian rubbed its hands together in anticipation, though to be honest I wasn't actually sure if the eldritch creature coiled inside me *had* hands. Agravane nodded firmly.

"Right, well, let's go get ready to stir up chaos."

CHAPTER 2

As it turns out, attending a rock troll coronation party isn't as simple as it seems. It's something like a mortal wedding and a coming of age ceremony all rolled into one. Guests are required to bring gifts, and will also be receiving gifts, and then there was the matter of food, attire, transportation and dealing with Agravane being forced to stay behind.

"The invitation says 'plus one', which means you can't come," I said, for about the third time, waving the piece of paper before Agravane. He snatched it from my fingers, read the thing over, snarled, and stalked back to his desk.

"Cal, are you allergic to arugula?" Yolanda asked, sitting at her own desk, hunched over a stack of papers. Supposedly, it was the survey to maximise guest enjoyment, but really it was just answering questions about food allergies, preferences for meat cooking and a whole concoction of questions regarding seating arrangement. I had looked at the document, which had arrived after I returned the invitation with my RSVP, and promptly handed it off to Yolanda.

"No," I said, laying my forehead on my desk. It had been less than twenty-four hours since Life had killed and cured me, and I was already certain my cold was trying to come back. Either that, or being soulless now manifested in the form of a massive headache. "My only allergies are to shellfish and a general dislike of anything to do with Worcestershire sauce. Oh, and anything cooked by vampires."

"No…food…from…vampires," Yolanda said while writing out the words. She went back to filling out paperwork and I attempted to get my own work done. My social media, despite reports from my assistant, had gone largely unmanaged. I tweaked my advert for the coffee I represented, altering the colours on the picture just a touch, then posted that and started a new campaign for Death.

"Cal," Yolanda said.

"No other allergies!"

"What about the gift?" she asked. I turned in my chair to frown at her. She fidgeted with the paperwork, snapping the pen she was using between her fingers when she squeezed it too tightly. Her cheeks tinged orange and she refused to meet my gaze.

"I mean…I've never attended a coronation before," I said, trying to be as tactful as possible. "What sort of gift *should* we bring?"

"Not popcorn," Yolanda blurted too loudly.

Rock trolls, given their affinity to rocks of all sorts, had a passionate love for salt. Unfortunately, salt was not really mined in Elsewhere, and I had to source all mine from the mortal realms. The first time I had taken Yolanda to the mortal realms, she had devoured a bucketful of eggs bathed in salt at our hotel buffet. Her absolute favourite was popcorn, the microwaveable kind that was overloaded with salt. I had started purchasing it in bulk to keep office drama down whenever Yolanda and Agravane wanted to watch one of their soap operas.

"Well," I said, "surely we can take some popcorn for us, right?"

Yolanda considered this suggestion gravely. She nodded once. "Yes, that would be good."

"Great, but we still need to get a gift?" I pulled up a web browser and started looking for information on gifts for rock trolls.

"How about a salt lamp?" Agravane asked, giving up all pretence of working and spinning around to face us. "It's still salt, but not edible."

Yolanda made a face. "Giving inedible salt…"

"You could always pretend that Cal didn't know how rude that would be, blame it on him." Agravane produced a fierce grin and his eyes gleamed.

I wondered, briefly, if I should protest being put up as a scapegoat. It seemed wiser to hold my tongue and keep looking at gifts online.

"That would be fun," Yolanda said, nodding. "But probably not a good idea since he is meant to be representing Life."

Agravane shrugged. "If you insist."

"How about we steer away from food? What about

shiny things? Gemstones, jewellery, that sort of thing?" I turned my screen around so they could see the fancy jewellery website I had found for a place not too far from Death's lands.

Yolanda rolled her eyes. "Rock trolls, Cal. Gemstones are common as dirt to us."

"And don't the dwarves hate you for it," Agravane muttered. I had given him sole control over the marketing account for one of several dwarf nations. It had absolutely nothing to do with the fact that I couldn't spell any of their names, let alone pronounce them. No, I just thought Agravane was the best candidate for this sort of thing. Truly.

"Okay, fine, how about a giant fluffy blanket?" I asked, half kidding. It hardly seemed like the sort of thing one would give to someone for a coronation. Yolanda, though, widened her eyes and leaned closer to my computer screen. She stared at the king sized plush blanket I had found for a decent price and I swear I could see actual glitter in her eyes.

"That would work," she said, her words breathless and weak, like I had just offered to give her a salt mine.

"I mean, are you certain?" I looked at the picture. It seemed like a nice blanket, but it was just a blanket. There were hundreds of them out there, nothing particularly special about this one except that it looked very comfortable. "It's just a blanket."

"It's a *soft* blanket," Yolanda retorted, as if that explained everything. Obviously, I didn't understand rock troll culture very well.

"If you say so." I had Yolanda pick out an appropriate colour—grey—and pretended not to notice when I saw she had added two to the cart instead of one. I ordered the swiftest delivery—which in Elsewhere was quite impressive—and left to go pack so I wouldn't be there when the item arrived and Yolanda had to explain the second blanket.

A few minutes later, Agravane poked his head into my flat. "Post's here," he said. "You want I should tip the pixie extra?"

"No, let Yolanda do it. Wouldn't want to ruin her fun." I considered two suit jackets, trying to decide which cut and colour would work best for this sort of thing. I sincerely hoped that my clothes wouldn't be ruined like they almost always were when I did special tasks for Life and Death.

"Black," Agravane said. "With the pinstripes. If you take grey, you'll be too rock coloured. We want you to stand out, not get swallowed by the crowd. And the red silk pocket square and tie set."

I finished packing while waiting for the delighted squeals from downstairs to die down. Agravane leaned on my door frame. Being tall, powerful and rather dangerous, his leaning was usually very intimidating. Now, it just seemed curious.

"You're staring," I stated, voice emotionless.

"You're being awfully nice. Any particular reason, or is this another side effect of your condition?"

I blinked, startled. Was I being nice? I didn't know. I thought I was being normal—at least, as normal as you can get in my condition, as Agravane put it—but it was difficult to tell. I had to rely on other people to gauge my emotional state, and often my assumptions were way off.

"I hadn't noticed," I admitted. "I thought I was just making Yolanda happy after having been dealt the blow that someone else is taking her place now that her father's dead. Oh. Right. Her father's dead. How did I forget that?"

"I gather they didn't particularly get along," Agravane murmured. He hadn't talked to his own family since I'd hired him, at least not anywhere near me or Yolanda. At least I now had family to talk to again, even if my mother did scare both Life and Death.

"Well, I'm all packed," I announced uselessly. Agravane snorted.

We went back down to the office to find Yolanda stuffing something suspiciously blanket shaped under her desk. She fiddled with her keyboard, a bright smile on her face.

"All set!" she said, the sound far too cheerful for any time of day, no matter if you had just got a blanket. "Now, we'll have to walk a bit to get to the transfer point, but it's not far and we should get to the Great Northern Ridge by evening."

"Transfer point." I rolled the words over my tongue. "We're not taking a wyvern?"

"Restricted airspace," Agravane said. "The Ridge is griffin territory and they hate intruders. They hunt in packs, too."

I winced. Maybe it was better I didn't ask questions anymore. Despite not being able to die, I really, really hated being killed, and being torn apart by giant birds with cat claws sounded like a terrible idea. Not to mention it would ruin my suit.

Agravane waved a slightly dejected goodbye as Yolanda and I left. I had a feeling the social media account was going to be flooded with pictures of Agravane playing games in the office when I got back. Still, I was more intent on Yolanda. She led the way through Death's lands with relative cheer, carrying her bag and the wrapped blanket with one arm while gesticulating wildly with the other. Her conversation was inane, flowing from popcorn production to the food allergy intake form, the trees and flowers growing at this time of year. The chatter increased the closer we got to the border and her expression became more animated, more intense.

Finally, we stopped at a large boulder that bordered the drive entering Death's lands. It was about twice my height and several times as wide, and I had always thought it a bit out of place with the natural landscape and well-cultivated estate. Yolanda fell silent, her movements stilled, and she stared at the boulder.

"So, we just sort of…" she stopped and took a deep breath. Her grey-green skin paled to become almost corpse-like and she tugged at the hem of her shirt.

"Hey, you okay?" I asked. Yolanda shrugged.

"When you went back home a while back, your family reacted well, right?" Her voice was barely audible.

"I suppose. Baz was certainly enthusiastic." I recalled the breath-stealing hug he had given me. My mother had been as phlegmatic as always, but I suppose she had been pleased, also, or she wouldn't have gone to such trouble to make me visit more frequently.

"Don't expect it to be like that for me." My assistant stared at the rock, her mouth pressed into a thin line. I patted her arm.

"If you want to leave, we'll leave," I said. "But we're going to show everyone what they've been missing. Just remember, Yolanda, you have family here. And those idiots? They can't hurt you anymore. They'll have to face me if they do."

Yolanda gave me a lopsided grin, tears welling in her eyes. "You're a good friend, Cal."

"Right, now, how do we actually get where we're going?" I stared intently at the boulder, trying to devise a door or portal or anything. Yolanda chuckled.

"Just hold your breath."

Then, without warning, she grabbed my wrist and pulled me forwards, striding straight into the boulder as if it wasn't a solid object and liable to squish me. I yelped, panicked, didn't manage to take in a proper breath before being pulled into solid rock, and nearly screamed into the oblivion.

Travelling through solid rock? Would *not* recommend unless you are a rock troll. It felt compressed, as if I was being squeezed from all sides. The pressure around me increased and the heat rose, as if I were travelling through the core of the planet surrounded by a bubble. My lungs were bursting, I couldn't see worth beans and I'm fairly certain I got grit everywhere.

No doubt about it, my clothes were ruined.

After what felt like aeons of being ground into dust, we emerged into light. I didn't even look around before falling to my knees and gasping for breath. Yolanda patted my back, which caused an explosion of dust from my suit. Finally, I could focus on something other than my lungs and saw only smudges.

"Glasses," Yolanda said. I pulled off the offending lenses and scrubbed them clean then slipped them back on my nose. The smudges resolved themselves into a whole pile of rocks. I suppose I shouldn't have been surprised; we were going to a rock troll party, after all. This particular pile of rocks was at the base of a narrow mountain trail leading up to a cave. There were tiny, scrubby trees dotting the landscape and a few patches of grass, but most of the greenery came in the form of moss and lichens. The rest of the surrounding scenery was much the same, with a massive mountain ridge stretching throughout the horizon as far as I could see. There were a few valleys between the peaks, populated with the larger versions of the trees, but mostly it was mountains.

"So...The Great Northern Ridge, then?" I asked, wobbling to my feet and dusting myself off. Yolanda, annoyingly, looked perfectly pristine, her jeans and t-shirt as clean as they had been when we had left. Some sort of rock troll trick, I imagine.

She nodded. "Yep. This was where I grew up."

I noticed that she didn't say this was home.

"Not many trees," I said pointlessly.

Yolanda sighed. "I'm fine, Cal. Now, come on, we need to go up there."

She pointed to the cave entrance and handed me our stack of papers before picking up both our bags. Apparently I was to lead the way. I brushed off more dust, hoping the trolls had a decent dry-cleaning service, then started walking up towards the cave entrance.

If you've never been to mountains that are still relatively young, geologically speaking, then it's hard to understand just how biting and thin the air can be. These particular mountains were still young enough to be tall and pointed rather than the smaller, smoother mountains one finds in Great Britain. Having been to the Himalayas on an unfortunate trip with Life, I could tell that these were not quite so steep, but they were certainly steep enough to have me trying not to gasp for breath by the time we reached the cave entrance.

I took a moment to straighten my suit, suck in a few lung-fulls of air, then put on my best In Charge expression and marched into the cave.

I don't really know what I was expecting from a cave populated by rock trolls. Maybe bare rock walls and floors, with a bit of dankness in the air. The caves belonging to the Order of Silence, a group of assassins bent on maintaining the balance between Life and Death, were much like that. These, though, were far more palatial.

The cave entrance outside looked like a simple collection of rocks with a gap to let people in. Inside, the entrance was carved into magnificent columns topped with gargoyles and creatures who lived in Elsewhere. The walls were decorated with brightly coloured mosaics depicting what I assumed were events from rock troll history. The mosaics had precious gemstones dotted throughout in quantities far more numerous than I had imagined. The floors were carved into massive polished tiles. The whole thing had lamps of reddish stone along regular intervals, the light inside giving a soft warm glow.

This entrance rivalled anything I had ever seen, including the mansions belonging to Life and Death. I gaped. I couldn't form a coherent thought, let alone a coherent sentence. The craftsmanship was astonishing and my mind was whirring with ways to take pictures and put people carrying cups of coffee here for a social media campaign.

Someone coughed politely.

I whirled around, nearly dropping the stack of papers in my hands, and found myself face-to-face with a rock troll in a poorly tailored suit, hands folded in front of him, legs spread, what I'm sure was a gun holstered under his shoulder. Had we been outside, he would have been wearing sunglasses. Definitely security.

"Welcome, sir," the troll said. He was about as tall as Yolanda with far more muscles, and his smooth, gentle tones did not match his physique at all. "May I see your invitation?"

"Oh, yeah," I said, again nearly dropping my stack of papers. I fished out the thick paper and handed it over.

"Ah, Mr. Calvin Thorpe, acting representative for Life, and his plus one. Um…your plus one?" The guard looked over my head, scanning the entrance. It was then I realised Yolanda hadn't come into the cave with me.

"She's around here somewhere." I went to the entrance and found Yolanda standing still at the end of the path, looking at the rock with watery eyes. "Hey, you okay?"

She nodded. Took a deep breath. Put on a smile that I almost believed to be genuine. Then followed me inside.

By the time we got to the guard, his jaw was as wide as mine had been a few moments ago. Only, he wasn't staring at the decor. He was staring at Yolanda. She ignored his look, casually glancing around at the mosaics and the carvings. "I should have brought you to the northern entrance," she said. "It's much nicer than this one."

I wasn't sure whether to laugh or agree or acknowledge the fact that Yolanda had just insulted her own people. Sebastian roused inside of me, taking a good look around. It quirked a brow at me and I shrugged mentally. Sebastian, surprisingly, stayed awake rather than going back to sleep, and fixed its attention on the guard still gaping at Yolanda.

"Is there a problem?" I asked, my voice low.

Sebastian growled.

The guard visibly paled, his grey-green skin turning the colour of a fresh corpse. "Um...well...it's just..."

"Speak!" I commanded, my voice ringing through the cavern entrance. With Sebastian active, there was an extra ring to my voice that sounded almost intimidating.

"That's Yolanda Rochefort, the former heir to the throne. She's dead." The guard hunched his shoulders, blinking rapidly, the invitation crushed in his hands.

"Are you dead?" I asked Yolanda.

"I don't feel dead," she answered, just as cooly.

"Very well then." I turned back to the guard, who was now completely paralysed with indecision. "Are you going to let us in? Or am I going to have to report back to Life—and Death, for that matter, who *employs* Yolanda—that we were turned away just because you didn't want to cause a scandal."

The guard straightened and fixed me with a nervous smile. "N-no. Welcome, Mr. Thorpe, Ms. Rochefort. I hope you enjoy the coronation."

His voice cracked on the last word.

Yolanda seemed to take pity on the guy, because she said, "I'm not here to take back the throne. I'm here to accompany my boss in acting as a representative for Life and Death."

That did not appear to reassure the guard. He tugged at his collar and rapped his fist twice on the massive stone doors blocking the entrance from the rest of the cavern system. There was a crack as the latch was undone, then the doors swung open on silent hinges and Yolanda and I were let inside.

"There's one victory," I murmured. She shrugged, studying the floor studiously. "Okay, where to next?"

Before I could pause to consider the answer, or even admire the carvings and mosaics along the hallway inside the doors, a tiny blur flung itself through the air and landed on my head. I felt claws digging into my scalp and whatever it was screeched loudly, the sound echoing through the cavern.

"No! Bad Tempest! We do *not* accost guests!" A small rock troll woman ran towards us, her hands outstretched. She was perhaps my height, her figure slim rather than muscular, her eyes blue rather than yellow or bright green. She wore a pair of dirty brown pants and a long white shirt, both covered with a leather apron. Her hands were covered in leather gloves which bore numerous scratches and patches, probably from whatever was perched on my head and trying to burrow its way into my skull.

The troll skidded to a stop right in front of me. "Oh, I'm sooo sorry! She just got away from me and I couldn't catch her and then she came out here and—" The troll had finally spotted Yolanda. Her mouth worked a couple of times, her eyes widening to almost comical levels. Then, with a squeal, the troll launched herself at Yolanda.

"Yollie! You're here!"

"Ah, yes. Hello, sis." Yolanda patted the other troll's back awkwardly. I felt as though I should say something to note the significance of that statement and my shock thereof, but the thing perching on my head leaned over and bit my ear.

So I screamed instead.

CHAPTER 3

olanda's sister, who I learned was called Katrina, absolutely freaked out and refused to stop fussing over my bleeding ear. She had hurried Yolanda and I to the aerie, where the trolls apparently kept an array of birds they bred to carry messages, or for hunting, or just as pets. The thing that had attached itself to my head was not an ordinary bird, though. No, Tempest was a miniature griffin.

The creature had the head of a small barn owl, with a large white face and feathers blending into the striped fur of a nearly black tabby cat. Her tail was stumpy and her wings bore the same tabby markings as the cat part of her body. Her claws, I had learned, were extremely sharp and left holes in my scalp.

My ear, though, was the real problem.

"It won't stop bleeding," Katrina wailed. She shoved another wad of rags at Yolanda, who replaced the now-red one on my ear with a shrug in my direction. "Oh, I'm going to get in so much trouble…"

"Maybe we should go to the infirmary," I suggested in a completely flat tone. I wondered if I should classify the sharp feeling in my ear as pain. Probably.

Tempest hissed, the fur on her spine sticking straight up. She was in a cage near the table and seemed distinctly upset by the situation. I would try to escape, too, if I had been cooped up in a cage. Though, there was something slightly unnerving about the gleam in her black eyes.

Katrina let out a squeak and tried her best to shrink into her shoulders. "Nonononono," she muttered, flapping her hands in distress. "If I take you to the infirmary, they'll know that I caused the injury and then I'll be in so much trouble and the aerie was my very very last chance!"

She burst into tears and buried her face in her hands.

I was generally terrible with other people's emotions, being so bad at my own, but even I know to be calm and understanding when someone starts crying right in front of you.

"I'm sure it's not so bad; they threw Yolanda off a cliff, and she's still here." I patted Katrina's shoulder in what I hoped was a comforting gesture. Yolanda's sister started crying harder.

"Well done, Cal," Yolanda said dryly.

I think it might have been the first time my assistant was actively mad at me to my face. Tempest screeched and launched herself at the bars of the cage, latching her claws around the metal.

"What happened?" Yolanda asked, rubbing small

circles over Katrina's back. "Last time I was here, you were on your way to being treasurer."

Given how much treasure the rock trolls had, that sounded like a significant job. To go from that to caring for the birds seemed like quite the change. I kept my mouth shut, though. I was nothing if not capable of learning from my mistakes. Even if that learning did sometimes take a bit of repetition.

Katrina snorted. "Yeah right. After you died—"

"Left," Yolanda snapped. "After they *tried* to kill me and I *left*."

"Fine. After you abandoned your family, Father did a thorough investigation of everyone who was in close contact with you, to see who could have helped you and that nymph develop a relationship. They decided that since my loyalties were already divided that—"

"Divided?" My mouth worked before I could stop myself.

Katrina waved a hand at her face, indicating her blue eyes. "Yeah. Half-human. So naturally I'd support a mixed pairing."

"Ah." I hadn't even realised that was possible.

Yolanda winced. "That's not *your* fault. And it's not like you have any contact with the humans of Elsewhere. Besides, nymphs and trolls aren't genetically compatible like humans are."

"Like that mattered. Father was furious with you. Cut off trading ties to the mountain nymphs entirely. Two cousins got exiled for admitting knowledge of your relationship. I got stripped of all my possessions and rank and had to work in the sorting yard to even stay in the tribe."

Tempest let out a growl, either in defiance at her captivity or in defence of her caretaker. Katrina's shoulders slumped and she sniffled loudly. I dug out a handkerchief and handed it over. She honked into it and shot me a marginally grateful look.

"Working in the aerie took *ages*. I first got promoted to a chef in the kitchens, then messed up some dignitary's food. Then I was sent on scouting duty, only I can't tell north from south. I only got to work in the aerie on a favour and now that's going to be taken from me as well. I'll be exiled, now."

"No you won't," Yolanda said firmly. She jabbed a finger in my direction. "Cal will fix it. Cal can fix *anything*."

"Uh, I can?" I asked. No one in the room seemed to hear me.

"You can come work with me." Yolanda nodded, a smile growing, obviously warming to whatever idea she had concocted. "I bet Death has something for you to do, if Cal doesn't."

Katrina squealed and threw her arms around Yolanda again. "Thank you, Yollie! Wait—did you say *Death?!*"

She pulled back and stared at her sister, eyes wide. Yolanda flushed bright orange and tugged at the hem of her shirt. "Oh, um. Yes. I work for Death. I'm Cal's assistant!"

Katrina whirled on me, taking a few safe steps back. "Oh, gems and stones, don't kill me!"

"Kill you? Why would I kill you?" I huffed.

"You're not…an assassin?" Katrina breathed the last word as though it was sacrilege just to think of such things.

"Certainly not! I do marketing. You have heard of the best coffee in Elsewhere, haven't you?" I pulled out my phone and showed her one of my more recent promotional graphics for the coffee I represented. Katrina blinked and squinted at the photo.

"I'm more of a tea person, really," she mumbled. Then, returning to her earlier point. "You don't kill people for Death?"

"No. I mean, not on purpose." I had to concede the last point, given my Reaper abilities. "And, really, being a Reaper doesn't mean I kill people, just that I walk the line between Life and Death and, well, that whole situation was an accident."

Yolanda sighed. Katrina stared. Tempest let out a sort of wheezing hack and coughed up what looked like the bones of a rat.

"Good girl!" Katrina turned to her charge and reached through the bars to stroke the griffin's head feathers. "That's what had you so upset, wasn't it? Yes, who's a good girl? You are! Yes you are!"

I tried not to draw any attention to the fact that my ear was only just now not bleeding by hiding the bloody rags behind me. "Do you know anything about marketing?" I tried to keep the conversation on track.

"No," Katrina said brightly. "I'm better at politics and financial planning. Give me a news website and an investment account and I'll double your money in a month."

Could be useful. I didn't really have a need for a financial advisor given that Death paid me remarkably well and I was also mostly immortal. But knowing about that sort of thing was helpful for planning marketing campaigns. Back in the mortal realms, I'd often consulted my marketing firm's political aficionado for tips on when to push certain celebrity and activist accounts. Here in Elsewhere, politics were a whole different animal than politics in the mortal realms. One with spikes and magical abilities and a really, really short fuse. Having an expert on hand would be useful.

"Very well, you're hired on a provisional basis," I said in my best boss voice. It was rarely effective, but Katrina seemed to enjoy it. "For now, you can start by giving me a rundown on the politics of the Great Northern Ridge Tribe. We're going to prove to them that throwing Yolanda off a cliff was a really, really terrible idea."

Katrina grinned, showing a set of perfectly aligned, bright white teeth. The smile was a little disconcerting, given the spark of rage in her eyes, but I let it be. She was on my side, at least.

We promised to meet up after the welcome ceremony, which was apparently starting soon. Yolanda suggested that we go to our rooms and I change my shirt. My ear, apparently, had bled more than a little bit on my collar. Before I could ask questions, like what in the world a welcome ceremony was, how bad my shirt was, whether there was a dry cleaner in the near vicinity or if I might get a cup of coffee before everything began, Yolanda had grabbed my wrist and dragged me from the aerie. Katrina let us go with a cheerful wave, Tempest screeching in the cage behind her.

I changed—good thing I'd packed several extra shirts—and then was dragged off to the Great Hall, again before I could ask about coffee. If the entrance to the cave system was impressive, the Great Hall was just beyond absurd. I stopped just inside the door and stared. Sebastian lifted its head and stared, too. It was just that astonishing.

The walls were carved from solid rock, with columns of polished marble stretching up at least sixty feet. The ceiling looked like it had been covered with a classical Renaissance painting, perhaps by Michaelangelo, only the paint was done in gemstones and the detail was carved from stone. The walls that were not columns had gargoyles at the top, with more carvings down below. All of it, as far as I could tell, depicted various characters from the rock troll history, standing in poses from paintings or wearing clothing found in the mortal realms throughout history. There were nooks in the walls bearing artefacts of various gaudiness: necklaces, statues, swords and the like. There were two other doors on either side of the far wall, both with massive wooden doors studded with gems. The furniture—benches and tables and chairs in a horseshoe shape along three of the walls—was all carved from the floor with slabs of stone, polished and intricate and potentially very uncomfortable.

As ridiculous as the decor was, the gathering of people in the room was almost more absurd. There were representatives from nearly every race and power I had encountered thus far in Elsewhere, with a few that I hadn't. There were Fae from both major courts, congregated on opposite sides of the room, giving each other nasty stares. There were aurai and satyrs, nymphs, elves and various other elemental-oriented creatures. There were vampires, though, thankfully, I did not recognise any of them. There were trolls by the dozens, some definitely rock trolls and others likely of a different subspecies. There were filmy beings that floated inches off the ground, creatures with hulking shoulders and some with steam pouring from their nostrils. Some beings were shrouded in shadow. Others were possessed of blue skin, indicating they were giants of various sorts. All were dressed in bright and elaborate clothing, the very best of the best, and holding drinks or food while they mingled about.

"Huh," I said, tugging on my vest. Beside me, Yolanda seemed to shrink.

"Maybe this wasn't such a good idea," she whispered, inching backwards.

"Nonsense. Just remember who you work for and the relative status of all these people to him."

Before Yolanda could respond, a creature that looked like a gnome sidled up to me and gave a decided sniff. "Your invitation, sir," he said, tugging at the curled ends of his beard. His accent was stuffy and his straight posture told me that he was likely some sort of servant here in the caves, which meant he would know everything and could make my life miserable in about a thousand different ways. I decided not to test the gnome and pulled out the invitation.

Immediately, that disdainful sniff turned into a formal bow. "We are honoured to have you, sir."

I opened my mouth to thank him when he spun around, slammed his foot into the stone, and sent a loud reverberation through the cavern. The noise and chatter died.

"Presenting Mr. Calvin Thorpe, Grim Reaper and acting representative for Life and Death, and his assistant Yolanda Rochefort." The gnome's announcement echoed for a few moments and a few people gaped at me in disbelief.

"I hadn't realised the invitations would include, ah, Sebastian," I muttered to Yolanda. She shrugged, looking just as dismayed as I thought I should feel.

Once the introduction had faded into silence, the crowd started talking again, some of them definitely muttering about the two of us; their pointed glances were quite obvious. Another gnome, this one with no beard and a tray of drinks, slid before Yolanda and I.

"No coffee?" I asked, frowning at the cocktails.

"Cal!" Yolanda hissed, snatching a glass of something suspiciously pink from the tray.

"If sir would like a coffee, I would be honoured to go make one," the gnome said with a formal bow, the drinks tray somehow never moving. Yolanda jabbed me with her elbow.

"Er, no. A gin and tonic will be fine," I said. Sebastian sighed happily as I was handed a generous portion of drink. My Reaper abilities much preferred that to coffee, which worried me slightly, when I actually thought about it enough to recognise the emotion.

"Well, well." A sly, smooth voice interrupted my thanks to the gnome and the poor guy was pushed to the side. A strangely attractive man was suddenly right in front of me, his clothes made of brocade and possibly a little too tight, revealing more muscle definition and skin than was commonly done in polite society. His hair was bright gold and swept to the side, the tone three shades darker than his tan skin. He had that sort of intent look of predators and smiled warmly while looking me and Yolanda up and down. "*You* just outranked everyone in the room. I can't believe we've never met before. I just *adore* powerful people."

I blinked. Frowned. Tilted my head. "Are you meant to be flirting with me?"

The man laughed and waved a hand. "Meant to be? No, Mr. Calvin Thorpe, I *am* flirting with you." He slid over my name like a caress, and I can honestly say I've never had my name sound quite so bizarre before.

"Back off, incubus," Yolanda snapped.

"Don't worry, my dear, I'm just as interested in you. The lost heir come back days before the new ruler is to be crowned? Absolutely delicious!" The incubus, which I belatedly realised was a creature who used seduction to sip life or power from a person, sidled closer. Sebastian started growling and a slightly yellow haze descended over my vision, telling me just how close to death the various guests were. The incubus licked his lips.

Then, before things could get even more strange, a knife flashed and pressed close to the incubus' ribs at the same time that his yellow nimbus flared neon, indicating he was moments away from dying. A woman, petite and muscular, her blue-grey skin shimmering in the reflected gemlight, her white hair done up in an elaborate braid, wearing a black silk sleeveless jumpsuit and combat boots, held the knife with a loving grip, her expression cunning and dangerous.

"Bartholomew, before you do something stupid, like antagonise a Reaper, why don't you go find someone else to play with, hmm?" The woman purred, sounding like a jungle cat. I felt my mouth fall into a pleased and probably sloppy grin.

Bartholomew, the incubus, took one look at the knife and the djinn holding it and left in a saunter, sidling up to some Faerie with hair of ice. The knife-bearing djinn tucked her weapon into a leather sheath at her thigh. She flipped a strand of hair out of her face, then looked up at me. "Hi, Cal."

"Hi, Neja," I said, and even my voice sounded happy, rather than the generally flat emotional tone. I was fairly tingling with happiness. "What're you doing here?"

Neja was a djinn who had tried, various times, to kill me while I was bearing Al Capone's soul during a favour for Death's cousin, the Taxman. The trying to kill me thing wasn't really her fault, and we had hit it off. Until my lack of soul combined with Al Capone's trouble-making tendencies had both of us backing off a more serious relationship. Since then, we'd become friends. Or something. I wasn't quite sure what we were. Neja was among the few people who knew that my soul was still out there, somewhere, and didn't seem bothered by it.

She was also a mercenary and bounty hunter for the Elsewhere elite and probably should have scared the socks off of me. She didn't.

Neja shrugged. "Oh, you know. Doing a job."

"Here?" Yolanda asked with a slight squeak. "But it's a coronation!"

"Yep, meant to be sussing out anyone who wants to ruin the fun." The djinn looked over Yolanda in her jeans and t-shirt and myself in my very nice suit with no bloodstains. "Are the two of *you* here to ruin the fun?"

"It's possible," I said. "We haven't yet decided what form our plans will take."

"Well, let me know what I can do to help." Neja fluttered her eyes and gave me a wicked smile.

"But your job…?" Yolanda looked taken aback, as if going against a job was tantamount to horror. Granted, she was the best assistant I'd ever had, so perhaps I shouldn't have wondered at her work ethic.

"My clients really should learn how to phrase their contracts better." Neja's grin sharpened. Then, she turned her attention to me and the grin fell away. Before I could ask what was wrong, Neja squished my face in her hands, turning my head from side to side, frowning as she examined me. Finally, after probably two minutes of scrutiny, she nodded firmly, released me, and said, "You need a haircut but seem otherwise healthy. Not having more problems with your lack of soul?"

"Just the occasional outburst," I said. "And some wonky emotions. Oh, and I had a cold the other day."

"Yes, well, everyone has wonky emotions. Yours are just louder without a soul to regulate them." Neja waved her hand dismissively. She threaded her arm through mine and led me deeper into the hall, Yolanda following closely behind. "We'll discuss how to get your soul back after the party. It's time we went on the proactive, not just reacting."

"Why do you care so much?" I asked, genuinely confused. She patted my hand.

"Because, Cal, I like you. I don't like a lot of people. That makes you my people, and I help my people. Also, you don't want anything from me. No wish magic, no unreasonable demands of employment, just me as me."

I tilted my head. "I recall wanting very much for your magic to stop killing me when we first met."

Neja snorted. "Yes, well, what relationships don't have their rocky patches."

I thought about pointing out that most relationships don't start with mostly unsuccessful murder attempts. I kept my mouth shut; it didn't seem particularly relevant given the rest of my life.

We edged deeper into the crowd of people. Most took a decided step back from us, their attitudes almost deferential. Few were willing to look me in the eye. Even some of the more powerful creatures in the room, those who had enough magic in their blood to make them relatively immortal, kept a safe distance.

"What is with everyone?" I asked when a Faerie covered in ivy skittered backwards, nearly colliding with a vampire.

"Oh, your title," Neja said casually, tossing her head. "It makes people nervous. Good for you finally admitting it, though."

"I didn't do it on purpose." I tried to reach for another gin and tonic, but the gnomes were somehow always just out of reach and getting farther away. Neja snorted and snapped a finger. Immediately, a gnome with a bright red beard appeared, holding a tray and trembling slightly. She took two drinks and the gnome vanished.

"Oh, thank you," I said. Neja whisked one of the drinks out of my grasp and handed it to Yolanda.

"Sorry, Cal, but I can't have you getting drunk. Who knows what chaos would come from that in an enclosed space. You'll stick to coffee from now on, okay?" Neja sipped her drink with the sort of arrogance that comes from many years of practise. Yolanda made a face at the glass she held.

"I can hold my liquor," I complained. It was too late, though. Before I could flag down another gnome, the entire cavern shook with a sound so deep that it reverberated through my bones.

Doom.

Silence fell, and the guests turned to face one of the doors at the other end of the hall.

Doom.

The sound grew closer, and I realised that it was someone pounding on a drum. The instrument must have been absolutely massive to make a sound that deep and loud.

Doom.

I yawned to pop my ears. Neja laughed quietly, then held a finger to her lips, eyes shining with humour. She pointed to the doors, which now swung open on silent hinges. From the shadows behind them emerged a being another head taller than Yolanda, with shoulders that would have made Atlas weep in jealousy. The creature wore a suit that had to have been ridiculously expensive, given the need for custom sizing all that silk. Its head was shining and bald, skin a deep grey, eyes like beacons of yellow.

A rock troll. It wasn't using battle magic to be larger, either, which was a little shocking. I didn't even know they grew that big. Beside me, Yolanda let out a groan that was probably loud enough to echo through the entire hall.

"Seriously?" she grumbled, the glass of gin shattering in her fist. "They picked cousin Eddie to be the next ruler?"

CHAPTER 4

By some bizarre stroke of luck that likely used up my entire quota for the month, no one seemed to have heard Yolanda's statement. The guests were either cheering or applauding the new leader of the tribe, and the only notice that we got was a female gnome, her hair done up in a beehive on the top of her head, cleaning up the pieces of glass at Yolanda's feet without a second glance.

Eddie, the giant of a troll taking Yolanda's place as ruler of the tribe, waved to the crowd like some celebrity rock god or athlete. He pumped his fists a couple of times, as though there were some upbeat background music. Oddly, the moment struck me as one that would actually go well with the strange music of Tiny Dinosaurs with Phasers. I vowed not to tell my cousin Baz, just in case the mortal music spread to Elsewhere.

Some things should be left well enough alone.

After a few more moments, when the cheering and

crowd-pandering became just a little too forced, Eddie waved his hands in a gesture to quiet the attendees.

"Thank you!" he called, his voice carrying over the crowd with ease. There was a strange quality to it, like it had been garbled and run through software designed to auto tune it. Neja winced.

"Surely your cousin could have got a better translation spell," she whispered to Yolanda. "Or, I don't know, actually bothered to learn the language of trade?"

Yolanda shrugged, looking even more despondent than ever. "No one learns English here. I had to take a correspondence course when I started working for Death. The tribes rarely bother, since they're already wealthy. If people want something from them, they come here, not the other way around."

"Yes, well, his translation spell is awful," Neja complained, perhaps a touch too loudly. We drew a couple of glares from our neighbours, who quickly looked at me and turned away, their backs stiff.

I was going to have to get used to being treated with fear and awe. It was very unusual.

"It's so good to have everyone here to celebrate such an important event. While the death of my uncle is super tragic, I know I can lead the Great Northern Ridge Tribe to total awesomeness and glory." Eddie raised his fist above his head again, resulting in another cheer. Most of the people making the noise, I realised, were rock trolls. Everyone else had grown tired of the show and were mostly clapping politely, or not clapping at all. I was in the latter group.

"Is that the spell making him talk strangely?" I asked Neja, keeping my voice low. Yolanda answered for the djinn, sighing dramatically.

"I wish," she said. "Eddie always talks like that."

"Part of my plans for this awesomeness," Eddie continued, as if he didn't see most of his audience growing bored, "is to open up trade that has been closed for a really long time. It's time we got back to interacting with the world, you know? Really embracing everyone around us. So, over the next few days, while the celebrations and games are going strong, I'm going to take some time and talk with all of the great delegations that came here so we can get to know each other better and work towards a new and brighter future!"

This statement met with slightly more enthusiastic applause from the audience, though I could see some of the parties—mostly the Fae—snickering amongst themselves. Trade was obviously most of the reason these people were here. I was more preoccupied with a different thought.

"Yolanda," I said carefully, keeping my voice barely audible, looking around to make sure that no one was listening. No one was, given that they were all trying to keep a very wide berth from me. "Is your cousin a hippie, or a cult leader?"

"Yes." She shook her head, wearing a long-suffering expression. "Welcome to the New Age. Try not to get converted."

Ah. Yes. Well, that did make things a little more complicated. I didn't quite know how, but there were definite complications. I sniffed and shoved my glasses up the bridge of my nose, wondering if one of the gnomes would bring me coffee. Coffee always helped with minor complications like dealing with a hippie cultist.

"Careful, Cal," Neja said, squeezing my arm more tightly than was strictly necessary. She looked amused, but there was a flash of warning in her eyes. "Even hippie cult leaders can be dangerous. I wasn't hired because the leader of the new order wants to spend time braiding everyone's hair and making flower crowns."

I patted my head self-consciously.

"Not your hair, Cal." Neja rolled her eyes. "Yours is too short."

Eddie was now exiting the stage, waving and smiling widely at the people. His drummers left the room entirely, but Eddie started mingling with the crowd. He seemed true to his word, greeting everyone with a smile that was, more or less, sincere. He never seemed to falter at an introduction or a stray state-ment, and he made his bulk seem somehow endearing rather than intimidating, like a giant teddy bear.

I didn't trust him.

Sebastian didn't either, for my Reaper abilities hadn't relaxed once since the rock troll entered the room, both eyes wide open and eldritch coils twisting and turning with slow intent.

"Can you relax, Cal?" Neja asked. "You're making people nervous."

"They were already nervous."

"Okay, you have a point. You're making *me* nervous." Neja shivered as Sebastian let out a low grumble. I tried to quiet my abilities, but it and I had never actually communicated before. Sebastian just sort of reacted to situations. The reactions had always been helpful, and enlightening, so I had never bothered to try and do anything about them. Frankly, I didn't even know if it was possible.

I closed my eyes and took a deep breath, focusing my attention on Sebastian. The interior of my mind, where it lived, was dim and lit with a deep grey light that came from nowhere I cared to investigate. I didn't spend that much time inspecting my own mind; it was a dangerous place and mostly caught up with thoughts that were either coffee-related or entirely cynical. The rest of it was taken up with Sebastian's many coils and twists. I had never seen the full creature, never seen its manifested shape as anything other than dark coils and two bright yellow eyes that matched the aura of a person's life. I wasn't entirely sure I wanted to see the entirety of Sebastian. Even being deathless, there were some things I preferred to avoid.

"Okay, Sebastian," I said inside my mind. "Can you do me a favour and try to tone things down? You're making Neja nervous, and if she's nervous, others are, too. We're here for Yolanda, okay?"

Sebastian fixed me with one massive eye. The other was fixed on Eddie, still moving through the crowd. Then, my Reaper abilities blinked at me and pulled back. I could still feel it moving inside me, ready to strike at a moment's notice, but I also knew that its restlessness was not visible to those magical beings who could sense such things.

"Thanks," I said, then opened my eyes.

Yolanda and Neja were staring at me, both looking disconcerted. Neja looked impressed; Yolanda looked slightly ill. "That was pretty cool," Neja said. "You just sort of darkened, then became normal Cal. Now, you don't look like anything other than a human in Elsewhere."

I frowned. "Don't I always look human?"

"Not always," was the unhelpful reply.

I quirked my brow in question at Yolanda, who shook her head and focused on the ground. I would have to text Agravane for an explanation. He was generally more helpful when it came to truths that other people didn't want to share. Of course, he would also be brutally honest in situations where that was not particularly helpful. It's why I gave him clients who appreciated absolute honesty. And those clients I just wanted to get rid of. I tried not to tell him which was which.

The people around us were still giving glances with various levels of nervousness, but they were no longer actively edging away. A group of Fae with flowers and vines woven through their hair and around their bodies shot me a dirty look as they walked past, but they stayed very far away. I was just glad Death's former pet cat, a grimalkin named Shakespeare, wasn't there. He *still* hated me for ruining his chances to start an all-out war between the courts. To be fair, I was just trying to be a good petsitter.

I was just about to ask how much longer we had to stand about when the crowd parted before us. It was an organic movement, one that just seemed to happen with the flow of the crowd, not through any particular intent. One moment there were people and the next, there was a clear path and Eddie was striding towards us with his hands in his pockets, a casual smile on his face. Given that he was so very tall, I had to crane my neck a little to get a good look at his expression. It was bordering on smug.

Sebastian hissed. I hoped the reaction didn't show outwardly.

Eddie stopped before me, put a hand across his chest and gave a weird bow, still smiling. "A real live Grim Reaper," he said, straightening. "It's super awesome to have you here."

The rock troll reached to take my hand in a more modern handshake when Neja slipped between us. "I wouldn't do that, if I were you," she said with a shrug and a cunning gleam in her eye. "Reaper abilities are activated by touch, and Cal hasn't had enough coffee today."

Eddie's eyes widened the tiniest bit, barely enough to be noticed. I noticed it. Sebastian did, too, and waves of satisfaction emanated from the coils. "No worries, man," Eddie said. "I totally understand. I'm a tea guy myself, cultivate some really nice puerh, but I'll make sure we've got coffee at all the meals for you."

"Er, thank you," I said, suppressing a frown.

"Wow, I'm just so hyped to be *talking* with you.

Reapers haven't been seen in centuries and, I mean, you guys were the original dudes!"

"I have no idea what that means." I looked at Neja, who just chuffed a laugh.

"You have to explain things literally to Cal," she said, slipping her arm through mind possessively. "He's very precise."

That wasn't quite the word I'd use, but it would suffice, I suppose. Neja patted my arm. Eddie looked at the joined limbs and blinked, the smile he wore never faltering for even a moment.

"Right. Precise. Well, Reapers were like, you know, the original power houses. The people no one messed with. You guys were badas—"

Someone coughed pointedly. It took me a moment to realise that it was Yolanda, standing just behind me. I turned to look at her and found her standing there with her hands on her hips, her expression unimpressed and unamused. "Cut the act, Eddie," she said. "Cal's not stupid, Neja doesn't care and I know you too well to buy any of your happy-go-lucky nonsense."

Eddie did two things following this proclamation: first, he looked around and noted that everyone in the hall was giving us a wide berth, all focused on their own conversations with distinct intensity; second, he let out a string of sharp curses. His voice no longer contained that serene note, no longer was quite so smooth with that weird auto tune quality. Instead, it was very distinct and spoken with an impeccable Received Pronunciation English accent.

Despite being English myself, I had not expected

that particular development. I blinked. Frowned. Wondered about that coffee. Sebastian growled deeply, but I had a feeling the sound was only meant for me. Frankly, I agreed with the great and terrible powers I held. I didn't like this one bit, and the added deception only made me like it less. I agreed with Neja. This hippie cult leader was definitely dangerous.

"Yollie," Eddie said. He was still smiling, just in case anyone glanced in our direction and found him disgruntled. "You're supposed to be dead."

"Yes, and you're supposed to be too far removed from the throne to rule," Yolanda snapped, voice low.

"As it turns out, a lot of people agree with my ideas," Eddie muttered. "Opening up trade, sharing with the world. Cultivating good will, importing healthier lifestyles. We're one of the oldest peoples in Elsewhere, and we're living isolated in the mountains. It's time to embrace both our past and the change that has come upon the world so we can share our knowledge and power with those who would seek us. Those who would wish to *understand*—"

"It's called marketing," I blurted out.

Eddie stared at me with something close to shock. I had probably interrupted him right in the middle of his rehearsed speech or tirade or whatever. Well, let's just say I have two areas of expertise: marketing and coffee. Apparently, I can't keep my mouth shut about either of them.

"So you converted Uncle Gino? And what about Cousin Beth? And Rosa and Linus and—" Yolanda was listing off names with venom.

"Okay, enough," Eddie growled, the pleasant expression slipping for a moment. He took a deep breath, held his hands at his centre in some sort of circle shape which I thought might be yoga-related, then smiled brightly again. "As I said, a great number agree with my ideas. I've even started language classes so everyone can learn the trade language without a translation spell."

So *that's* why his accent was so precise when he wasn't talking like a stoned hippie from the seventies. Yolanda did not appear to find this information helpful, or good. She looked as upset as I'd ever seen her, and if I didn't know better, I'd say she was going to clock Eddie right across the jaw.

"And what about Katrina?" Yolanda asked. Eddie snorted and appraised her, taking in the casual clothes, the anger simmering in her eyes, the snarl on her lips.

"What are you doing here, Yollie?" he asked. "Did you come to try and usurp my position?"

Yolanda growled, the sound almost as dangerous as Sebastian's growl. "I'm here as Cal's assistant."

This time, Eddie laughed, the sound echoing loudly through the cavern. A few people threw alarmed looks in our direction. Neja glared at them, though, and they all turned away. Eddie wiped a stray tear away, still chuckling. "You must be joking. *You?* In a position as important as working for a Grim Reaper? Ha! Never have I heard such absurdity, and I was there at your tribunal hearing!"

Without warning, the air stilled. The quiet drone of other conversations fell away, replaced with a crackling energy that set the hairs on the back of my neck standing on end. Neja reached for a knife at her belt. Sebastian chuckled darkly, seemingly the only one of us pleased by this turn of events. Before my eyes, a nimbus of energy gathered around Yolanda. There was no mistaking it as anything other than magic. The only problem was, rock trolls didn't *have* magic except in the form of their battle magic.

Yolanda breaking out her battle magic in the middle of the Great Hall? That would be bad. Monumentally bad. And yet, I would not have stopped her for anything.

Eddie snapped his hand out and wrapped it around Yolanda's throat. His smile was still vivid, but it had turned a shade brittle. His eyes were just this side of crazy. "You would use your battle magic *here*? Against me? We were right to have thrown you off a cliff. You wouldn't have lasted a year as leader!"

Yolanda scrabbled at Eddie's hand, her magic spluttering away, her anger replaced with fear. Neja tightened her grip on my arm, nails digging into me through my suit. Then, she backed away.

I got the message loud and clear.

More importantly, though, Sebastian got the message.

Whatever the creature had done to dampen its presence to the outside world vanished. I could feel it writhing inside me, unfurling its coils and stretching its head high, those yellow eyes furious. The shadows inside me were still too dark to see it properly, which was probably good, as the tiny part of me that could feel things normally was cowering in a ball with fingers in ears.

Sebastian snarled, the sound vibrating through me. My vision darkened, the colour leeching out of everything until all that was left were the auras of yellowish gold that surrounded each living being, indicating how close they were to dying. Eddie, if I had my way, would be very, very close to dying.

"Release her." My voice was two notes deeper than before, and it promised a great deal of pain.

Eddie let Yolanda go without question. He bowed deeply and formally, though I had the distinct impression that the weight of my power bearing down on him forced him to bend. If I pushed a little harder, I could bring him to his knees. The thought pleased me.

"You will not harm my assistant," I hissed. Eddie visibly paled. "And if anything happens to Yolanda or any of her family while I am here, even if it is nothing more than a stubbed toe, then I do not care about consequences; I will release my power to hunt through these caverns and turn them into ruins as a reminder to the next thousand generations that you do not harm me or mine. Are we understood?"

"U-understood, my lord," Eddie said, voice trembling. Sebastian gave him one last hiss then retreated. My vision returned to normal. I tugged at the cuffs on my shirt then adjusted my glasses.

"Yolanda has not returned to claim your throne," I said with a disdainful sniff. "She has far more important things to do with her time than worry about such matters. We will remain for the remainder of the celebration, as we had intended. Now, I am going to my rooms to rest."

I would have turned on my heel and stalked away, but Neja caught me in her hands before I could so much as shift my weight. Without preamble, she put her hands on either side of my face, pulled me down to her and kissed me soundly.

I think I melted.

A minute or more later—I lost track of time—and Neja released me with a satisfied grin. "Good man, Cal," she said, patting my arm absently. "Good man."

Then, she sauntered away.

Eddie and all the others in the room watched me with a mixture of wariness and awe that was both disconcerting and gratifying. I fled the room before I could think about that particular combination of emotions too much. I didn't think I would like the answers.

CHAPTER 5

I tried to piece together my thoughts after Neja's out-of-nowhere-but-not-unappreci-ated kiss and the resultant stares from the assembled dignitaries and came up with only incoherent sludge. Yolanda had to tug me in various directions to get back to our suite of rooms. Once there, I would have been perfectly content to collapse on my bed and relive that kiss for a while, but alas, it was not to be. My plans for relaxation almost never happen, so I shouldn't have been surprised at this particular interruption. However, when a mass of feathers and fur flings itself into your face just as the door is opened, though, one cannot help but be surprised. Given that this was the second time this had happened in one day, however, I did manage not to scream.

Barely.

"Tempest! Bad bird!" Katrina rushed forwards to detach the griffin from me as best she could. The crea-ture had latched its claws into my shoulder, piercing through my suit, and merely hissed at Katrina. I think she was laughing.

"Stop," I said, waving away the rock troll. "Pulling at her will only tear a larger hole in my suit and I *like* this suit. I would really rather not to have to have it sent for repair so quickly after having put it on."

Katrina blinked at me, then looked to Yolanda for either clarification or confirmation. My assistant just nodded, her expression long suffering. "Cal is very particular about his suits."

I sniffed. "Yes, well, puncture holes are far easier to mend than tears. My tailor's fees are rather high, and I really do not want to order *another* suit for at least several more months. Now, do we have coffee?"

"Um, it's in the kitchen by the—"

I didn't bother listening to Katrina's full directions, only turned in the direction of the excellently appointed kitchen and began the wonderful process of preparing my coffee. I did not care that it was late afternoon, that we were meant to be at a banquet in a few hours, only that I get my coffee. The rock trolls did quite well with their guest quarters, mixing modern convenience with intricate carvings and a great deal of shiny gems. It was relatively comfortable, but more importantly, it had a coffee-maker in shiny stainless steel right in the middle of the counter. I cupped the drink in my hands and inhaled, letting my mind empty of everything but that tantalising scent.

Then, once I had taken a sip and felt mildly more grounded, if a little out of balance with a griffin perched on my shoulder, getting her tail into my ear every few seconds, I returned to the sitting room where Katrina and Yolanda sat on a couch. They looked a bit unhappy. Rather, Yolanda looked as though she'd like to wring the neck of anything that came too close, and Katrina had her arm wrapped around herself for comfort, her expression distressed.

They both studied me while I sat on a chair that was not nearly as comfortable as it pretended to be. I shifted my weight. Nope, it was worse.

"Tempest likes you," Katrina said after I pummelled a cushion into submission.

"I beg your pardon?" I asked.

"She never sits on people's shoulders. Not any trainer she's ever had, nor any troll or client who has tried to handle her. Miniature griffins are notoriously difficult creatures. They make absolutely wonderful guard animals, trackers, even messengers or pets, but they can be very testy about who they trust." Katrina shrugged. Tempest chattered something next to my ear, rubbing her face against mine, getting feathers up my nose.

"Another economic change from cousin Eddie?" Yolanda asked drily. "When I was—when Father ruled, griffins were used as messengers and messengers only. There was no selling them for guards or pets or whatever. And the miniature ones? Never. Too high strung."

Katrina wilted just a touch.

"Relax, Yolanda," I said, just a touch more firmly than I had intended. "Things change. And, you said so yourself, you're not interested in taking back the throne. Therefore, let your cult leader cousin make his changes, try to win the hearts of the masses. That's not why we're here."

Yolanda huffed and crossed her arms. She glared at the floor and scuffed her foot against the coffee table. Being made of stone, it just endured the attack, whereas I think my furniture would have wobbled and broke. "It's never going to work."

"What is?" Katrina asked. "Eddie's plans? Because he's really smart, Yollie. Even some of his more radical ideas seem to make sense when he explains them in detail."

"It's a bad idea," Yolanda spat. I was astonished. I had never heard Yolanda so angry in the entirety of my knowing her. My hand wobbled slightly. I set down my coffee before I spilled it and Tempest took the opportunity to launch off of my shoulder and wing around the room, eventually settling on a nook high in the corner, which was probably meant for some sort of sculpture. I fingered the holes in my suit and found them fairly small. Thank goodness the griffin only had domestic cat claws.

"You can't expect your people to stay isolated forever," I said. "I mean, look at how much you learned while you've worked for Death. Right?"

"It's not about learning, Cal," Yolanda grumbled. "I have no problem with learning. It's…it's the way that Eddie is talking. Like he wants to spread his ideas no matter the cost. Like he…"

She growled in frustration and shook her head.

"He never explicitly said he wanted to go to war," Katrina murmured. "Not that I've heard. And no one else is talking that way. We're mostly just happy to have language training and appliances. But…it's definitely possible."

"What's possible?" I asked. "I do not understand."

"Rock trolls—and other species, too—have battle magic because we're very, very good at battle," Yolanda said. She fixed me with a frank, intense stare. I returned the stare with a still-confused one of my own. I had seen her in her battle form when she rescued me from vampires, and while it was scary, it was hardly surprising. Most of Elsewhere had some sort of magic. "The various tribes of rock troll live hundreds of miles apart because if we were any closer, we would be engaged in near constant war. Rock trolls are good at any number of things—mining, learning crafts, building—but we are exceptional warmakers. The leaders of our people are meant to keep us from war, not encourage it, because otherwise we would turn the world red with blood, regardless of what stood in our way."

I was beginning to get a grasp on what was happening, on why Yolanda was so upset. Eddie's speech had been, on the surface, a means for promoting trade and understanding between the rock trolls and the rest of Elsewhere. Under the surface, though, was the desire to spread their culture and traditions. At all costs.

Katrina let out a small sound that was somewhere between a moan and a sob. "They should never have exiled you. This is bad. I can't believe I didn't see it! Me, who prides myself on knowing politics and financial schema. Is this why he put me in the aerie, where no one else would talk to me? It must be! Oh, this is really, really bad."

"Couldn't we just depose Eddie? Put someone else in power?" I asked. "Sebastian would be thrilled to do it."

My Reaper abilities grumbled agreement.

Katrina frowned and Yolanda shook her head. "Ruling families must be picked from the royal bloodline." Katrina scoffed at me as though this were obvious.

"Human rulers are notorious for being deposed or executed and a new bloodline put into place. It doesn't work the same here?"

Yolanda shook her head, threading her fingers together. I had the sudden urge to go make her a bowl of popcorn so I could remove that sullen expression from her face. "The leaders of the rock troll people are those weakest in battle magic. Those of us who have to find other solutions to problems because we can't fight without losing. It's a hereditary trait."

"Every so often," Katrina continued, as though she rarely got the chance to expound on rock troll history and genetics, "a time of war does come upon the tribe. Then, the strongest warrior mates with the heir to the throne and the current leader is killed. A warrior gets to be in charge for a short period of time, but ultimately power stays with those who can't fight."

This political schema actually explained a great deal about Yolanda. And, honestly, it made a lot of sense. Strange, convoluted sense, but sense nonetheless.

I took a large mouthful of coffee. "Let me guess, Eddie is a warrior."

Both rock trolls nodded.

I realised then just how serious Yolanda's offense had been to her people. She had, willingly or not, doomed them to losing their ruling family. Which, if they were as war prone as these two suggested, would be a problem.

"Right. So. Who would be the heir—besides Yolanda? You, Katrina?" I gestured with my mug to the small troll, who flinched back.

"Half-human," she squeaked. "Doesn't work. No one would accept me. I don't even *have* battle magic."

"So you're basically the pinnacle of leadership in rock troll society." I nodded. The others stared at me. "Okay, new plan! We're going to still make everyone realise how awesome Yolanda is, but we're also going to get rid of cousin Eddie. And put Katrina on the throne."

Yolanda, for the first time since the invitation had been delivered to me by Life, smiled her signature wide grin, showing all her teeth. "I like this plan."

"This is a terrible idea," Katrina muttered from between her fingers, which now covered her whole face.

Tempest screeched and beat her wings. I didn't know if that was agreement or just annoyance that she'd been forgotten in all of this. I took it as agreement.

I stood and clapped my hands together. "Right! Who wants popcorn while we plan?"

Katrina gasped. "You have *popcorn*?!"

"Cal is a good person," Yolanda said, nodding and smiling. I wasn't entirely sure how providing popcorn made me a good person, but I wasn't going to argue with brownie points. Actually, arguing with brownies in general is a bad idea, since they are responsible for much of the well-functioning domestic life in Elsewhere.

After I made popcorn—and more coffee—and doled out large bowls to all parties concerned, we got down to business. "So," I said, sipping my beloved drink. "How does one actually...depose? Is that the right word? How do we depose Eddie?"

Yolanda made a face then stuffed her mouth with popcorn. She chewed with firm anger and swallowed with an audible gulp. Bad news, then. "It is not possible. Eddie is the next in line, if the others of the blood-line have given up their right, which I believe they have."

Katrina sighed, stuffing a handful of popcorn into her mouth. She chewed swiftly, but when she spoke her words were still nearly unintelligible. "Beth lasted the longest, but he wore her down."

"How?" I asked. "And please, both of you, finish chewing before you answer. I have more popcorn; there's no need to rush things."

She blushed a burnt orange and hunched her shoulders. "Ah, well. Sorry. Um...let's see, Eddie is smart. He knows that he can't win the leadership by fighting, so he mostly just persuaded people to accept him. Offered language classes. Proposed new trade routes. He made people like him, and when he approached a few of the bloodline about making a bid for the throne, they just agreed. Beth didn't for a long time, but he won her vote in the end. I think there was something else involved, though, because she won't tell me why. She transferred to one of the scouting parties soon afterwards and spends most of her time outside the complex. She says she finds it peaceful, but she was a renowned gem carver before and hated the outdoors."

Yolanda growled, the sound deep in her throat. She had her fists clenched on her knees and was completely ignoring her popcorn. I nudged her leg with my foot and tilted my head. She took a deep breath, eventually releasing her fists. She still did not eat the popcorn.

"That the family was so easily won with language and new trade...it is proof of how far things have fallen," Yolanda grumbled. "Once, you could have offered my father an entire mortal salt mine and he would have still stood by his principles."

"It's complicated, Yollie," Katrina murmured. "Our isolationist ways—all the trolls' isolationist ways—mean that we're stagnating while the rest of Elsewhere moves on without us. Look at you! You're so much smarter than you were before. You work for *Death*, Yollie. The power in that alone is nothing to sneeze at."

Yolanda rounded on her sister, gleaming white teeth bared. "You *agree* with Eddie?"

"Oh, don't snarl at me," Katrina snapped. Even nearly half Yolanda's size, the younger Rochefort sister was not at all cowed. I liked her for it, partly because Yolanda was *scary* when she was angry. It happened rarely, but was not something to ignore. Even Agravane didn't provoke Yolanda into anger, despite his own power and strength. "I told you that Eddie is smart. He's promising innovation to entice people into his fold. Access to other creatures. Better food. Better quality of life. New, shiny things like popcorn. The fact that his particular brand of crazy also includes pushing the 'superior' culture of rock trolls onto everyone and subjugating anything inferior doesn't really register with most people. They see the good, none of the bad."

Yolanda growled again, but apparently had nothing more to say. She shoved her hand into her bowl of popcorn and ate a fistful. Katrina's shoulders sagged, but she copied Yolanda. I finished my coffee.

"You haven't answered my question," I said. "How do we get Eddie off the throne?"

"Once a ruler is sworn in, they are in until death," Yolanda snapped. She glowered at the stone furniture. I understood the implication. Of the three of us, I was the only one who could really kill Eddie. It would be easy, with Sebastian curling around my innards. I hoped it wouldn't come to that, though. I hadn't been lying when I told Katrina that I was a marketing agent, not an assassin.

"Yeah, but Eddie isn't sworn in yet." Katrina's words were soft, barely audible, but they managed to send shock waves through the entire room. Even Tempest, who was grooming herself and clacking her beak noisily, froze and fixed an eye on Katrina. Or her popcorn; I wasn't really certain.

"There's not enough time," Yolanda protested.

"Enough time for what?" I asked, sensing that this was potentially significant.

"Harold the Mad was denounced in an hour," Katrina countered.

"Harold the who? And time for what?" I wondered if they were even listening to me.

Yolanda sighed heavily, sounding like an emotional teenager. "There's a law. It's rarely used, because enacting it is ridiculously complicated, but it could prevent Eddie from being sworn in."

Katrina straightened and glared at her sister before turning to me with a pleased expression. "Basically, if Eddie proves himself incapable of the responsibilities that holding the throne entail before he is sworn in, a member of the bloodline can declare him incompetent and denounce him. Then, the assembled dignitaries vote and a new ruler must be chosen. Harold the Mad was the last one to be denounced, and it took him less than an hour to start a riot that nearly had the entire population cheering for war over the loss of a pet mouse. Granted, this was several hundred years ago, but the precedent exists."

I felt my mouth twitching and was uncertain whether I was trying to laugh or cry. I decided not to ask about the pet mouse and instead focus on the more relevant detail. "If we can get Eddie to declare his intent for war, then, he'll be out?"

Katrina winced, but nodded. "More or less."

"Great. How do we do that?"

Yolanda grumbled something around a mouthful of popcorn. I tilted my head.

"Sorry, didn't catch that."

"I said, you could just annoy him into showing off his battle magic," Yolanda said.

I was fairly certain that she meant to be insulting, but it wasn't an impossible idea. I would just have to disregard all my training as a marketing agent trained to appeal to all people and channel the more bothersome side of me. After all, everyone has a bothersome side, and when I so chose, mine could be a real doozy.

It was better than breaking out my dark and dangerous and murderous side. Far better.

Of course, there were difficulties with this plan as well, but no one would have to die. I tilted my head back to stare at the carvings on the ceilings, a distinctly unpleasant depiction of trolls climbing a mountain and claiming it as their own, the bodies of their enemies at their feet. My options were few: I could either be as annoying as possible, ignoring most all of the socially acceptable rules and forms and epitomising my most absurd traits in the hopes that Eddie would find me bothersome enough to loosen his control on his battle magic; or, I could kill. I knew which was the better route.

"Very well." I nodded firmly. "I will do my best."

CHAPTER 6

Our plan to annoy the daylights out of Eddie until such time as he attacked me with battle magic began the next morning. Per our coronation week schedule, provided on helpful large print card-stock with gilded capital letters, the various dignitaries would be taking a tour of the cave system, led by Eddie himself in a bid to show how great and awesome—his words, not mine—the rock trolls really were.

I wore a suit and patent leather shoes. Yolanda dressed in sensible jeans and sneakers, sporting an oversized Tiny Dinosaurs With Phasers t-shirt that I hadn't even known she owned.

"Baz?" I adjusted my pocket square, already knowing the answer.

"Your cousin is very fond of this band," Yolanda said, picking at the hem of her shirt. "I don't like the music much, but they make a comfortable shirt. Plus it will drive Eddie crazy. He hates pop culture, especially mortal pop culture."

"Baz will be so pleased to help in our endeavours." I pulled out my phone and took a picture of Yolanda, who posed obligingly, then sent the image to my cousin. He was still in the mortal realms until the negotiations were over, but managed to chat with Yolanda and Agravane almost daily. How my cousin had managed to grow so close to my office staff, I did not choose to ask. I suspected it had something to do with my Netflix account, as there were a suspicious number of films that I had never seen showing up. Either that, or the daily messaging had something to do with it. He also pestered me to text him constantly. I appeased him with pictures on a more occasional basis. We were working on it.

Before Yolanda and I could venture out to meet the diplomatic group, the door to our suite burst open and Katrina ran in, Tempest flying in her wake. She was breathing heavily and her eyes were wide, almost terrified.

"Um, hi," she said, her back pressed against the door. Tempest chirped cheerfully.

"Hello," I said. "Are you joining us on the tour?"

"Oh, uh, no. I'm not allowed. I was just…can I hide out here while you're gone?"

Heavy footsteps sounded in the hallway beyond our door and I quirked an eyebrow. Yolanda let out a sigh. "What did you do to annoy the guard?"

Katrina shrugged, her eyes looking anywhere but at us. "I may have…well, I may have accidentally spilled a barrel of griffin food on them just before feeding time. Raw meat is a difficult smell to disguise, and, well, the cage doors weren't closed as securely as usual."

I snorted. "You set a pack of tiny cat birds on the guards? Why?"

Tempest trilled, swooping around the room, as though immensely pleased to have taken part in this particular endeavour. She made two circuits then began to dive for me. I held up a hand.

"Don't ruin the suit!" I snapped. "I need it for our plan."

To my surprise—or, at least, what should have been a surprise but was really more like a hiccough—Tempest wheeled backwards and landed gently on my shoulder, her talons gripping only enough to hold her in place. Katrina stared at me.

"She likes you," Yolanda said.

"Eddie won't like that. The griffins are hugely valuable, partly because they're so volatile. They're really useful, too. But if they bond to you, that's it, they won't work with anyone else." Katrina scratched her arm nervously. "That's why they put people like me in the aerie, because the birds aren't likely to, ah, well, get attached."

Tempest made a sound that was somewhere between a chirp and a purr, rubbing her head against my ear and knocking my glasses askew. I sighed and righted them. Then, just because it seemed like a good idea, I tickled her under her beak. She closed her eyes and the purring sound got louder. "Well, we are here to annoy Eddie, after all. Let's just try not to set any *more* griffins on me. I can only carry one."

I started for the door, feeling unbalanced with the extra weight on my shoulder. Then, a thought occurred to me. "You'll get out of this tour for now, but at future events, you should be with us, so people can see you. You'll be my unofficial griffin handler, and if that doesn't work, I'll make you coffee bearer. Just…you won't be accepted by anyone if you're hiding in the aerie, Katrina. Or my rooms."

The rock troll hunched her shoulders and wrapped her arms around herself. She looked so small compared to Yolanda, and even smaller since she was trying to disappear into herself. But she bit her lip and nodded. "I'll try," she said.

"Good," Yolanda said. She wrapped her arms around her sister and squeezed. Judging by the squeaking sound, Katrina was having her organs rearranged. "You'll be a much better ruler than I would ever have been."

She released her sister, patted her on the head, and followed me out the door. We were greeted by a harried looking troll wearing a dress of indiscriminate grey. She eyed Tempest, looked at me, shook her head, said nothing, and led us to the Great Hall, where we would meet up with the rest of the tour.

Thanks to my extra fussiness when it came to dressing that morning, as well as the arrival of Katrina and Tempest, Yolanda and I were the last people to arrive. Fashionably late it would be called in the mortal realms. In Elsewhere, it was mostly just rude, but I was apparently powerful enough that no one could do anything about it. Neja was hanging out with a group of very angry looking people in leather armour. She nodded at me, then went back to talking with them. I would catch her up on the plan later. Eddie was standing with a group of vampires, smiling widely and gesturing broadly while they eyed him with barely concealed suspicion. He faltered ever so slightly at our arrival, and his eyes widened almost comically at the sight of Tempest on my shoulder. He said something to the vampires and wandered over to us.

"Good morning!" Eddie said, using that awful translation spell again. "It's super awesome to see you!"

At this banal greeting, the attention of the other guests wandered away from us, likely already tired of Eddie's cheer. He waited a few more beats to be certain, then somehow frowned at me while never once dropping his smile. "Where did you get that griffin?"

"Tempest?" I asked, reaching up to stroke her feathers. She preened in delight, spreading her wings and buffeting me in the head as she did so. "She latched herself to my head when I first arrived and has since taken to following me around. You know, you should be more careful about who hangs out with your griffins. They're very valuable, see. You wouldn't want them to get attached to someone just out of the blue."

Eddie studied me, looking for something in my expression. Whatever it was, he didn't find it, because he just bowed, that infernal smile still on his face. "Consider her a gift, from the Great Northern Ridge Tribe to the Grim Reaper."

"Wow, that's super nice of you," I said, my tone as

bland as ever. There were some benefits to being without a soul, and straight-faced sarcasm was one of them. If Eddie realised I was mocking him, he didn't let on. Instead, he turned to Yolanda, who was picking at a carving with her nail, dropping tiny crumbs of stone to the floor.

"Good morning, cousin. I didn't think you would be interested in a tour of our home, since you are already so familiar with it." Eddie was wearing that false smile again, and doing it with great aplomb. He glanced at her shirt. "And in such strange attire, too."

"Oh, you haven't heard of Tiny Dinosaurs?" I asked, waving at Yolanda's shirt. I pitched my voice louder so the surrounding diplomats would definitely hear us. They started paying rapt attention, though perhaps they had never stopped. I was unused to this whole fame situation and didn't quite know how people were going to treat me. I rattled on about the band despite having only heard half of one of their albums before giving up, much to Baz's disappointment. "They're all the rage in the mortal realms. My cousin—he's been recruited by Life and Death to be Justice—is a huge fan."

By the surreptitious mutterings that people started producing, I was fairly certain that obscure punk band with questionable music was going to be getting a sudden upswing in sales. Part of me cringed at the thought of hearing their music all over Elsewhere, but I reminded myself that we were here to annoy Eddie and show how awesome Yolanda was. Sporting merch from the newest band to sweep the magical stage would be a good start.

"Ah…" Eddie started. He obviously wasn't prepared to argue about music this early in the morning, if at all. Before I could start debating the merits of the band—which started and ended, in my opinion, with their comfortable clothing, but don't tell Baz I said so—someone pushed through the crowd of gathering dignitaries.

"Yollie?" The voice was deep, rumbling, and sounded like it should be narrating audiobooks for a small fortune. At the sound of her name, Yolanda froze, every muscle in her body going stiff, her skin paling. She took a breath that rattled like a death knell. Immediately, I was on guard, Sebastian rearing up and looking around for the threat.

Yellow auras, some brighter, some dimmer, surrounded the people and the rest of the colour leeched away until everything was desaturated. Tempest screeched and fled to a plinth housing a stone gargoyle. Several people around me—two Fae, a vampire, a goblin, some sort of creature made of greenery, and what looked like a fire elemental—stepped back. This left room for the owner of the voice to step forwards, his attention fixed wholly on Yolanda.

Even if I hadn't known about Yolanda's doomed relationship with a mountain nymph, I would have guessed that this guy belonged in the outdoors. He was tall, almost as tall as Yolanda, built like a woodsman, had a tan that was probably achieved by almost never stepping indoors, and wore clothes that were both stylish and practical. He was attractive, certainly. Strong, definitely. And he walked right past Sebastian and me without a second glance, going straight to the still-frozen Yolanda like he had seen a ghost.

"Yollie, it's me, Boulder," he said, resting his hands on her arms. She didn't flinch away, but neither did she move. "I…I thought you were dead!"

Yolanda gulped, eyes flicking to me in panic. I took this as a sign she wanted me to step in and make things less awkward. Sebastian took this as a sign to growl. Deeply.

The rocks around us rattled, a few pieces of tile cracking with the sound. Boulder finally dragged his attention away from Yolanda to look at me. He yelped, then stepped in front of Yolanda as if to protect her from me.

Right there, without even requiring a conversation, I approved of the guy. Sebastian must have too, because it gave an approving nod and retreated with a sound of satisfaction. My vision returned to normal, Boulder's bright yellow aura vanishing. I tugged at the cuff of my sleeve, then held out my hand.

"Hello, I'm Cal Thorpe. Yolanda's boss. I take it you must be the infamous Boulder about whom I have heard almost, but not entirely, nothing. Pleasure to meet you," I said.

Boulder stared at me, jaw agape. He looked like he was going to say something, so I waited patiently. After a few moments of this, I looked at Yolanda over his shoulder. She was no longer frozen, but blushing fiercely, her hand over her mouth as she looked between me and Boulder.

I didn't get a chance to say anything further, because Eddie, looking far too smug with himself, clapped his hands and called out, "Alright, everyone! Time for the super awesome tour. Now, if you'll all follow me, we're going to head through the hall towards the archives. The initial cavern of the Great Northern Ridge Tribe was carved several thousand years ago when Nigel the Great broke off from the Strong Peak Tribe and…"

I stopped listening after we passed into the hallway. Eddie sounded like every tour guide at every tourist site I'd ever visited in my life. Even with the translation spell, he had that chirpy, annoying ability to over explain everything and provide all the information you didn't want to know. If there was something actually of interest to me, I'd pay attention, but for now, I was perfectly content to watch Boulder and Yolanda just in front of me.

Yolanda was walking with her arms close to her side, trying very hard to avoid being drawn into Boulder's grasp. The mountain nymph, on the other hand, was doing his best to sidle closer to her, casting glances between Yolanda and myself before inching ever closer. Sometime during this awkward dance, Tempest flew up, settling on my shoulder again. She gave an indignant squawk.

"Yes, yes," I said, patting her while she pulled on my hair with her beak. "I'll warn you next time Sebastian emerges."

The griffin muttered, but settled onto my shoulder again, kneading my suit. I returned to studying my assistant, who was acting very strangely, given that she had once promised to be mated to this nymph.

"Well, Yollie?" Boulder whispered after the tour had been going on for a few minutes. A blue-skinned giant was the only person close by and she looked as though she would fall asleep on her feet with the way Eddie was droning on. There was little chance of being overheard. "Where have you been?"

Yolanda shrugged and muttered something.

"What? I didn't catch that."

"With Death," Yolanda said, a little louder. She hunched her shoulders and shoved her hands into her pockets.

"So you *did* die?" Boulder gasped. He looked horrified, checking her over as if one could tell by looking whether a person had died or not. Unless you were a zombie—or a vampire—I didn't think it was quite that simple. "They told me you'd fallen over a cliff. They told me you'd *thrown* yourself over a cliff."

Yolanda glowered at her cousin's back while he waved expansively at the mosaic on the wall, depicting some sort of epic quest. Either that or a theatre troupe performing really badly. "They lied," she spat, more vicious than I'd ever heard her. This trip was revealing quite a number of darker facets to Yolanda's personality. I reminded myself not to get on her bad side. "Our relationship was discovered and I was disowned, removed from the family lineage, and instead of granting me a banishment, they threw me off a cliff. My *father* threw me off a cliff."

I winced. Perhaps it was a good thing we hadn't returned here until after his death. Boulder looked horrified, hands covering his mouth and his eyes bright with tears. "So you didn't…jump? You weren't ashamed?"

"*Ashamed?*" Yolanda hissed. The sound carried perhaps a bit too well in the stone hallway and gathered a few interested looks. I cleared my throat pointedly and the overt interest subsided. Boulder shot me an alarmed look over his shoulder and tried to walk faster. Yolanda resolutely stayed where she was. "I could never be ashamed of you, Boulder. I loved you!"

"Then where have you *been?*" he demanded.

"Death found me in the Instant of Death and offered me a job," Yolanda said, glaring at the mosaic on the wall. The tour was moving ahead with us as the stragglers. There were two guards behind us, though, who were inching closer to try and usher us along. They smelled suspiciously like sausage; I caught Tempest looking at them with strong intent.

Yolanda finally started walking, her shoulders hunched. Boulder fell in line beside her. "So, what, you were his assassin? Stationed at some distant corner of the mortal realms?"

She shook her head.

Boulder placed a hand on her arm. She stopped walking. "Then why didn't you *contact* me? You could have written. Called. You could have sent a messenger bird, for crying out loud. Anything! Instead, it's been years and I just thought you were dead. I had to be bribed to work with these creeps again, after what I thought they'd driven you to do."

My assistant, strong and cheerful, sometimes terrified, but always up for facing the most difficult of situations that I somehow dragged us into, blinked away tears. Her chin wobbled.

"Oookay, I think that's enough of *that*." Neja's intervention was, as always, perfectly timed. She slipped her arm through mine and looked between Yolanda and Boulder. "I spend one morning with the honoured warriors of Valhalla and you nearly get Eddie to squeal with glee in my absence. Stop making Yolanda cry, or you'll have to deal with Cal."

Boulder stiffened and looked at the djinn in alarm. He looked at me for a fraction of a second then nodded with what I think was meant to be a polite smile on his face. "You have my sincerest apologies, Reaper. I did not mean to—"

"Oh, nonsense," I said, waving a dismissive hand. "My name is Cal. The Reaper business was an accident, though I'd prefer if no one here knew that. I'm Death's marketing agent, not his assassin."

If his presumed-dead girlfriend coming back to life hadn't astonished Boulder, I certainly had. He stopped walking altogether, gaping at me as if I'd suddenly developed a fish for a head. We were stared at by the guards a few paces back and started walking again to catch up with the rest of the tour.

"You're Death's...*marketing agent*. And Yolanda is...?"

"My assistant." I pushed my glasses up my nose and did my best to glower at him, though I've been told that I'm not very good at it. "And if you do one thing to hurt her, I'll smear your name for the entirety of Elsewhere to see, so that not one day will go by without someone using the name Boulder as a verb for making a huge, massive, irreversible mistake. Then, I'll string you up to a wyvern and let Agravane—my other employee and former member of the Order of Silence—deal with you. And if that doesn't work, we'll revisit those Reaper abilities."

Boulder visibly gulped. "You got it," he squeaked.

I smiled. "Good. Now, you can help with our plan to prove what idiots these rock trolls were to get rid of Yolanda, here."

To his credit, Boulder took the change in direction very well. Neja patted my arm. "How do we plan on doing that, dear Cal?" she asked, her voice sugary sweet and hushed.

"We're going to annoy Eddie into using his battle magic on me," I replied. "Oh, look, the kitchens! Time to start Phase One."

CHAPTER 7

*I*t really was altogether too easy to get on Eddie's nerves. He was, on the whole, very capable at hiding his displeasure, but I have been informed that I have a special talent at bringing people to their knees in frustration and despair, figuratively speaking. At least, I'd never witnessed anyone actually falling to their knees because of me, but I had been the target of several attempted murders.

As the tour passed through the kitchens, I distracted the head chef with questions about their coffee. Where it was sourced, how it was harvested, how it was roasted, how it was ground, brewed, etc. I then debated the relative merits of dark roast and medium roast with the guy, firmly stating that the coffee brand I represented was superior to the brand he served in his kitchens. (To be fair, he had a very respectable Italian roast, but I represented the best coffee in all of Elsewhere, so it was difficult to compete.)

Throughout this exchange, Eddie tried to get me to move along, as I was holding up the tour, but he underestimated the power of coffee. By the time I was wrapping up the debate, I had drawn the elves, giants and nymphs into the argument. The Fae had tried to bring tea into the equation, but that quickly got dismissed as an entirely different category of drink with entirely different requirements, not even considering the black versus herbal debate. Boulder turned out to be very knowledgeable about coffee growing, and my approval of him went up a few notches.

Then, as I thanked the chef for his time—and carried a to-go cup of coffee—Tempest decided that she needed to be in on the fun. She leapt from my shoulder to a station where a beleaguered young troll was cleaning fish. The troll panicked, as was only appropriate when a small, dangerous winged predator appears out of nowhere, and backpedaled into a gnome carrying a tray of appetisers for the diplomats on the tour.

The appetisers went flying.

Tempest flew after them.

She had a severed fish head in one of her front talons and reached for the flying appetisers with the other. I'd never seen a creature so eager to get to food before, and certainly not one of her size. It was impressive and a little frightening and I wondered how Death felt about tiny griffins in his kitchen. His dogs, Mischief and Mayhem, might like Tempest. What a terrifying thought.

Then, breaking into my musings and with enough

force to knock over a small building, the griffin slammed straight into Eddie's face.

Yolanda snickered. Neja buried her head in my shoulder to hide the laughter. Even Sebastian seemed pleased by this turn of events. Boulder alone looked a little horrified, his hands clasped over his mouth and his eyes bugging out as he stared at the carnage of appetisers, feathers, cat fur and a severed fish head.

During this incident, the other diplomats were waiting on the edges of the room, either talking with one another or just standing there until the tour moved on. As soon as Tempest collided with Eddie, though, they fell silent.

"Oh, dear," I said, my voice emotionless. "How terribly unfortunate. Your suit looks like linen, and isn't that such a bother to clean. I hope nothing sets before you can get it to the cleaners or it really will stain."

Neja was visibly shaking now, gripping my arm tightly and laughing into my shoulder. The muffled sounds would have been concerning if I hadn't known she wasn't choking. Yolanda was pointedly looking somewhere else, though I saw a flash of her pleased expression before she grabbed an apple and stuffed it into her mouth. Boulder looked between the three of us, uncertainty flashing in his eyes. Eventually, he edged closer to Yolanda in a show of solidarity.

"It's fine," Eddie said, a very distinct growl in his voice. Tempest screeched and fled to my shoulder, where she proceeded to groom out bits of cheese and cracker from her fur and feathers. Eddie glowered at the griffin, then looked at me. He put a hand over his heart and bowed. "A suit is nothing in comparison to having the Grim Reaper attending my coronation, and I'm sure it was an accident. Though, might I recommend some training for your new, ah, gift?"

I pushed my glasses up my nose and tried not to narrow my eyes. He was playing this very well. Several other diplomats and important people were nodding, smiling at me and offering various unhelpful hints for training birds or cats.

I hadn't considered just how much these people wanted to pander to me. Frankly, I also hadn't considered Neja's words from the night before, that I, with one announcement of my official title, outranked everyone in the room. Yes, I was aware of the massive being writhing within me. I was aware just what being a Reaper entailed. I was even aware of people staring at me, paying attention, as they would any employee of Life and Death's. I just hadn't realised what being a Reaper truly meant for my social status.

I was a marketing agent. Public relations officer. Representative of my bosses.

Extremely powerful being who holds the actual balance of Life and Death in my fingers? Yeah, no.

But these people, even the Fae who still hated me after things had gone down between the courts due to my interference, looked at me like they wanted something from me, even if it was just acknowledgement. It would get them nothing but acknowledgement by others, yet still they craved it. Even Eddie.

I could probably annoy him until the cows came home, but he would still just bow and scrape. Unless I actively attacked him, then there was a very good chance that this plan would fail. He wouldn't dare use his battle magic on me. I was just too powerful, too influential. I was nothing more than a human with Reaper abilities that had developed due to two mistakes, one each from Life and Death. I was average, and yet these people were salivating for my attention. It made no sense.

I was just Cal, a product of my circumstances, not this...being that people should admire just because I was me. I had worked hard to earn my position as marketing agent, hard enough that Death hired me. Then, all because a couple of mistakes by cosmically powerful beings and suddenly I'm a force of the universe, a creature of balance and terrible power. It was something I had not quite come to terms with.

And it was currently ruining all my plans.

The whole point of having me be the focus of Eddie's ire was that I could be injured, even fatally so, and it wouldn't matter. But if he would never dare to be so disrespectful, then I would have to get someone else involved. Make someone else the target. Someone who could get hurt.

I put on what I hope passed for a pleasant smile. "My apologies, Eddie. I'll talk with Katrina about how to properly train a griffin."

Eddie straightened. Already, the kitchen staff were cleaning up the mess, though none dared to brush off the suit of their illustrious leader. "Katrina?" Eddie was also wearing a pleasant smile, but he looked a little discomfited.

"Yes, Yolanda's half-sister?" I said, gesturing to Yolanda, who stood with Boulder, both of them now eating apples. "She seems very capable. Knows a great deal, and not just about griffins. It would seem she's been trained in politics and finance! Isn't that just the most useful thing?"

Eddie clenched his fist. His smile brightened, this time so much that it looked like it might shatter. "We have a wide range of training and career paths here in the Great Northern Ridge Tribe. Coupled with our extensive trading paths, it's what makes us poised to be a nexus for all people of Elsewhere."

A blue skinned giantess muttered, loud enough for all to hear, "Yes, that's why you still use translation spells."

Well, well, it would seem I wasn't the only one who didn't trust cousin Eddie.

Perhaps realising that he was losing control of the crowd, Eddie clapped his hands and gestured to the hallway beyond the kitchens. "Now, if you'll follow me, we're going to look at something that has never before been shown to anyone outside the Great Northern Ridge Tribe: our mines!"

Eddie clapped again and grinned as people whispered about this opportunity to see where the gems and precious metals were mined. I wasn't the only one who had been impressed with the trolls' decor; many of the attendees eagerly followed Eddie, leaving the kitchens behind without a second glance. The blue giantess took enough time to quirk a brow at me before she, too, left. Neja linked her arm with mine and pulled me along, Yolanda and Boulder drifting behind us. Our guard made up the rear, though he was sure to keep a reasonable distance, especially since Tempest was eyeing him with interest.

"An interesting plan, Cal," Neja said once we had passed into the hallway. "You expect your ability to annoy people to send that one over the edge?"

"With a little help," I said. "Even I can't be *that* annoying, after all."

"I wouldn't be so sure about that," the djinn replied. She tossed her hair and batted her eyes at me. I think she was teasing me, but it was difficult to tell with Neja.

"This is wrong," Yolanda grumbled from behind us.

"I thought you liked the plan," I protested. I had worked hard on that plan and thought it was a very good one, thank you.

"Not the plan, Cal. Going to the mines," Yolanda said, still grumbling. She was shuffling her feet along, glowering at the walls. Boulder was right beside her, his brow furrowed.

"What's so wrong about the mines?" he asked. "You used to tell me all sorts of wonderful things about them."

"Yes, but you never *saw* them," Yolanda replied. She bit her lip. "They're...not meant to be seen by outsiders. The mines are our great secret. They're the first and last things that we're taught to defend. They're important to us."

The walls were growing wider, taller, as we drew nearer to wherever these mines were. The air grew warmer, too, as though someone had turned on the heater and then added an extra furnace and a bonfire, just for good measure. The mosaics along the walls diminished, until it was smooth, bare stone looking out at us. The change from artistic and detailed to that vast blank space was unnerving.

"If they're so sacred," I started, dropping my voice, "then why is Eddie revealing them?"

The closer we got to the mines, the more discomfited I became. My hackles rose and Sebastian started roiling around, its great eyes wide open and alert. Tempest dug her claws into my shoulder, likely piercing the suit, but I couldn't bring myself to scold her. Even Neja looked nervous, fingering the knife at her belt.

"I wish I knew," Yolanda whispered.

The hallway veered suddenly to the right, the blind corner opening up into a vast cavern. The tour group came out at the top of the cavern, with paths and branches and tunnels littering the whole thing, all the way down to the ground, which was lit with massive fires and what looked like tiny vats of molten metal, but were probably giant vats of molten metal. All along the cavern, rock trolls emerged from tunnels, pushing carts or carrying boxes of glimmering dirt and rock. Uncut gems and raw ore, likely. Tiny ant-like figures of trolls worked the forges down below, turning rock into slag and slag into metal, metal into just about everything. Jewellers' wheels turned constantly, polishing up the gems until they shone in the firelight.

It was a hugely impressive operation.

What sent shivers down my spine, though, was the singing. The songs weren't like any music I'd ever heard before. There was no melody, no harmony, no lyrics that I understood. There was just words, chanted at different pitches to the same rhythm, coming from the mouth of each rock troll no matter what they were doing. Frankly, it was eerie and I was tempted to turn around and go right back to the kitchens.

It was also a little beautiful. I understood why Yolanda considered it so important.

"Song spells," an elf said, peering over into the depths. "I thought the art had died out an age past."

Eddie looked ferocious in the reddish light of all the fires, shadows dancing under his eyes and along his jaw so that he looked like he were a being ready for bloodshed and war. The smile, that same cheerful hippie cult leader expression, now looked vicious, dangerous. "Not dead, just treasured, kept alive here while the world forgot about the art."

Sebastian hissed deep inside, something in the not-quite-music setting the eldritch being on edge. I didn't disagree. This magic, whatever song spells were, was a potent thing. I could practically taste the power floating through the air, and I instinctively knew that it could be used for more than harvesting gems and ore. It could be used to unify an army, to sweep it across the lands, and only the strongest magic could keep it at bay.

"Such long-dead secrets belong to all beings of Elsewhere, so that we might revive the art," the elf said, clutching a necklace at her throat as if it would provide strength or protection from the fierce visage of the rock troll leader.

"And I am willing to trade for them," Eddie said peaceably, folding his hands in front of him as if he had not a single care in the world. As if he weren't about to become solely in control of a weapon that could change the face of the world. No wonder the leaders of the rock trolls weren't meant to be warriors. "We rock trolls have done our sacred duty and kept these song spells alive, so that one day we might share our secrets with the world, prove to them that we are not the foolish people we are thought to be. That rock trolls are worthy. Respected. Isn't that super awesome?"

The cheesy words thrown on to the end could do nothing to hide the fact that Eddie's ambitions went far beyond the guise of a cheerful hippie, hoping for equality and peace between the peoples of Elsewhere. He may have hoped for trade. He may have wanted to learn about various cultures and species, and to have them learn about rock trolls in return. There was something more, though, and if any of these diplomats denied it, then they were blind fools.

There was silence for a moment, and I saw several people looking at each other, exchanging glances and whispering in ears. The elf cast a wary glance at Eddie before talking with her peers, and both Fae courts were huddled together, their murmurs lost beneath the steady thrum of the song. Goblins, giants, elementals, beings I had no name for, all whispered together. They all saw right through Eddie, of that I had no doubt. I may have been the most powerful in name, and I considered myself a relatively intelligent guy, but these were trained diplomats. They knew just as much about manipulative schemes as did any marketing agent.

They were also greedy.

I saw the gleam of excitement in the eyes of many as they spoke. How many of them wanted to acquire such spells and gain more power? To preempt the rock trolls and go to war?

The more I saw in this place, the more I became convinced that deposing Eddie was our best option. Sebastian huffed an agreement.

"Cal?" Neja whispered, eyes wide. "Do something!"

Ah, right. Time for a distraction.

"Well, it's a little out of tune. Doesn't really do anything for me." I yawned, for good measure. "Is there somewhere else on the tour? I'd like to see your library. Or maybe a view of the mountains? Or your cargo distribution centre?"

Everyone turned to gape at me, even Yolanda and Boulder. The nymph had drawn closer to the edge, peering down into the depths like the song called to him, drew him in. For all I knew, it did. He was a mountain nymph; if that was anything like his tree-hugging cousins, he likely had an affinity for the mountain. He could probably sense better than anyone what that spell song was doing.

"You...do not find the spell song impressive?" Eddie

asked, frowning. It was such a change from his smile that—in the light—he almost looked nicer.

"Not terribly," I said with a shrug. "Then, I've grown up listening to The Beatles, Dire Straits, Pink Floyd, Bach, Beethoven, Mozart...you know, the highest pinnacle of mortal music. Even Tiny Dinosaurs with Phasers is more interesting than this."

Whispers started up again, but this time they were questioning. If the Grim Reaper didn't find the spell impressive, then what did that mean?

"Surely you've just never encountered such powerful magic before," Eddie insisted, smiling broadly again.

I shrugged again, accidentally jostling Tempest. She latched her beak onto my hair, thankfully missing my ear. I didn't need my wound to reopen and bleed everywhere. What sort of message would *that* send?

"Oh, I have," I said. I kicked a pebble over the edge. "I mean, Life and Death tore me to pieces on more than one occasion, and I'm still here. And then there was that time in London, when I...well, let's just say the dreaming giants and exousia are still trapped."

Saying it like this sounded a whole lot more impressive than any of these things had actually been. Yes, I had intentionally trapped both a giant and angel in an eternal game of chess, but that was more through cunning than brute strength. And the Life and Death tearing me apart thing? I only survived because I couldn't die. It had still hurt. A lot.

Eddie didn't seem to know what to do about this. He shifted his weight from foot to foot, looking at the gathered guests. They were more interested in me than the song spell now, watching with interest. I didn't like the attention, but better this than a whole bunch of magically inclined beings trying to get their hands on the highly volatile weapon just being casually slung about below our feet.

I decided not to mention to Yolanda and Katrina my theory about Eddie. Maybe I was wrong. Mostly, I just didn't want to put anyone else in danger.

"So," I said, "onwards?"

Then, I turned on my heel and led the tour out of the caverns, gesturing to Yolanda. "My assistant is very familiar with these caves, as she was the heir apparent prior to Eddie's ascension. I bet Yolanda can tell you where they hide all their treasures."

Yolanda blinked at me. Then, she caught sight of her cousin, now taking up the rear of the tour, the guard at his side. Eddie looked an inch away from murdering someone. Yolanda brightened, smiled her best smile—which is infinitely better than mine—and nodded.

"Yes, I can show you the most interesting parts of the complex. Who wants to go see the place where Great Uncle Felix got his toe stuck in a drainage pipe?"

The tour only improved from there.

CHAPTER 8

According to Neja, the welcome ceremony and the tour were just prologue, events to keep people interested while straggler diplomats arrived and event plans were finalised. They were meant to be little more than fluff, entertaining and yet little involved in how the Great Northern Ridge Tribe would be perceived under their new leader, despite the obvious interest in the song spells. What came after the tour, though, was the start of what would be some very complicated political manoeuvres meant to impress the realm of Elsewhere and solidify Eddie's rule.

It all started with a banquet.

"Wear the blue tie," Neja said, lounging on my bed while I stood there in my white shirt and socks, trying to determine the rest of my attire for this banquet that was meant to be supremely important. Neja was wearing a dress in stark black that went to the floor. It had a slit up the side that let her grab the knife I was certain she carried, and a neckline that I appreciated a fair bit, though I could have sworn there was the hint of another knife hilt showing there. Her shoes were her standard practical boots.

"Isn't this meant to be a formal event?" I asked, holding up the tie in question in the mirror. It was bright, drew attention, and did not at all go with the dark greenish-grey of my suit. Maybe I should just wear the standard black. "Should I wear white-tie?"

Neja laughed. "The fact that you actually *have* white tie attire is so you, Cal."

"Well, Yolanda did say this was a coronation, so I figured there would be formal events and usually, that means—"

"Cal, stop. Wear the pinstripe suit and vest with the blue tie. If you show up too formally for this banquet, people will think you care about this particular coronation. Elsewhere fashion works differently. It's less about how people perceive you, and more about how you perceive the world around you." Neja gestured to her own dress. "In this instance, I am acknowledging that the event requires a formal dress, but my boots say I am more interested in being comfortable, and the knives—don't think I didn't notice you admiring me, Cal—say that I am perfectly happy to skin anyone who gets too close, regardless of who I offend.."

I hesitated while doing up the buttons of my vest. "Does that mean me, too?"

Neja laughed. She stood, the dress swishing pleasantly, and crossed over to me. She plucked the tie from the top of the chest of drawers and slung it around my neck, tugging me closer. She kissed the tip of my nose before releasing me enough so she could tie the tie with deft, practised movements. "Nope," she said. "You can get too close if you want."

I probably gave her a rather goofy grin when I hoped to be suave, but I couldn't much bring myself to care. Sebastian started making a strange rumbling sound, coiling over itself inside me. It wasn't a growl, and yet Sebastian didn't *seem* upset. I looked down at my torso as if that could help me diagnose the sound, realising a moment later that Neja was also staring.

"Is...Is it *purring*?" she asked. Her eyes were wide.

I blinked. Considered. Examined Sebastian. My cheeks heated. "I think so, yes," I said.

"Huh." Neja looked confused, though the corners of her mouth quirked up a bit.

"So what's the big deal about this banquet?" I asked, partly to change the subject and partly because I really didn't understand what the big deal was. I'd been to banquets before and they hadn't seemed quite this significant.

"This shows how well Eddie can handle different delegations, different needs. How well he can show off his own wealth and the skills of his people while also seeing to others' needs. Food choices only make up one part of the situation. You can't feed a banshee the same food you'd give to a nymph, and that's not even taking allergies into consideration. But the really important part is all about seating people in the appropriate place. You can't have the Fae courts next to one another, but neither can you sit them near the allies of opposite courts. That's just the Fae. Not to mention you can't seat creatures of lesser standing too high in the hierarchy, or you will be seen as foolish. You have representatives from dozens of races here, who all require such considerations. A banquet on this scale requires meticulous and detailed planning, or you'll offend people who could become important allies."

I frowned. "I don't really care where I sit. As long as there's good food."

Neja patted my shoulder. "Yes, Cal, I know. You're relatively low maintenance. But other people don't know that. And everybody will be wanting to sit closer to you so they can be associated with your power. The closer to the Reaper, the better the standing."

"I don't want to be a pawn in Eddie's games," I grumbled. "I just want dinner." I shoved my cufflinks into my sleeves and twisted them into place. Then, I put my shoes on and shuffled out to the main seating area, where Yolanda and Katrina were already waiting. Boulder was likely in his own rooms getting ready with the rest of his people. Tempest was sprawled out on the back of the couch, wings twitching merrily as she dreamed. Everyone looked more at ease than me.

Yolanda was wearing pink, some bright, flowy number that looked decidedly too cheerful for this sort of occasion. I don't remember her having packed anything so colourful, so I assumed it was a recently acquired piece purely for Boulder's benefit. Katrina wore green, a dress she absolutely swam in. It looked like it had been several sizes too large and taken in by someone whose experience with sewing was that the pointy end of the needle went into the fabric first.

I must have been staring, because she blushed a burnt orange. "I…don't often get new formal clothes. Why would I need them, being in the aerie? But since you invited me to this banquet, I got this. It's hard to find second-hand clothes that fit me, being half-human and all."

"You look good in green," was all I could manage to say. Katrina's blush deepened.

Neja sighed. "Ignore Cal's lack of tact, love. Now, do as I tell you." She leaned over Katrina and whispered something in her ear. The young rock troll looked up at the djinn with hope, then nodded. She clasped her hands together, bowed her head, squeezed her eyes shut and muttered something so quietly I couldn't hear. After she finished muttering, she clapped her hands three times. There was a sudden flash and after I blinked away the aftershock, Katrina sat there looking very pleased.

Her dress fit her perfectly, and looked almost regal.

I tilted my head at Neja and she shrugged. "Wish magic can be useful, sometimes. Such a simple ritual only works well for small things—and I have to be in the room—but it's worth it, sometimes."

Yolanda rose from the couch and wrapped her arms around Neja, squeezing her. "Thank you," she said.

Neja squeaked in response. Yolanda let her down and winced, muttering an apology.

"Shall we go, or do you think we should be fashionably late?" I asked, interrupting the gratitude permeating the air. All three females turned to look at me, some more annoyed than others. I held up my hands. "I truly don't know the answer," I said. "Please don't mess up my suit."

Katrina snorted a laugh. "Come on, Cal, you come with me. I'll guide you through all the politics."

I gratefully took her arm and walked with her to the banquet hall, pretending I didn't see her fussing with her skirt and smiling widely as we walked. She became increasingly more formal the closer we got to the banquet hall.

It was different from the Great hall that the welcoming ceremony had been held in; the ceilings were barrel-shaped, with carved stone beams running end to end. There was a massive fireplace on either end of the room with smaller braziers throughout to dispel the darkness. There were candles on the many, many tables, but no other light, giving the massive room a sort of homey feeling. The tables were round, covered in white tablecloths, set with square white plates and silverware of varying sizes for varying sorts of hands. There were name cards at each spot, and trolls dressed in smart uniforms along the edge of the room to take the guests to their assigned spot. It was like a pub had been made enormous and posh and, frankly, I enjoyed it.

When I entered the room, I saw that there were perhaps sixty or so people already there, mingling about and ignoring the polite directions of their guides to their spots. They all turned to look at me, quickly turning back to their companions and whispering loudly.

"No one wants to look at you too long in case you

take offense," Katrina whispered in my ear. Behind me, Yolanda was scouring the crowd, likely looking for Boulder. The mountain nymphs were nowhere to be seen, though, and I could practically feel the disappointment radiating off of her.

"Cal is not so good at figuring out what's meant to offend him," Neja said. She waggled her fingers at a couple of people with greenish skin and they immediately stiffened and flitted away. "Dryads. So touchy. They hired me a while back to do a job, bring back some renegade teenagers, and you'd think I tortured those kids the way they all look at me, now."

"Did you?" I asked.

"Of course not!" Neja snorted. "I just told them if they didn't come with me, I'd make them sit through an hour-long documentary on the logging industry. They came quickly enough after that."

"Oh, my," Katrina said, putting a hand to her mouth. From the inelegant sound that escaped, I got the impression she wasn't hiding her shock, but rather her amusement. "You're a political nightmare, but you sure are fun."

Neja looked pleased by that statement.

One of the guides approached, bowing low. "Welcome, sir, ladies. If you would please to follow me, I will take you to your seat, most honoured guest." The troll stayed bowed, not bothering to look me in the face even though we were of a height now that he was bent over. I wondered if that were an uncomfortable position, and how long one could stand like that before back pain set in. I decided not to ask.

"Okay," I said instead, curious where they would seat me, now that the importance of such things had been explained to me. I hoped that it was close to the fires; the stone room was a little chilly.

The troll wound through the tables, not even giving the other guests a second glance. Neja looked around, watching everybody, as if she knew precisely what they were thinking and planned to use it in her schemes. Yolanda and Katrina were close at hand, as if the guide would leave them behind if they strayed too far. I believed he would, too, and likely on Eddie's orders.

Finally, we stopped. There was a table before us, nowhere near the fireplace, but right in the centre of the room. There were tall braziers situated at intervals around the table, almost separating it into its own bubble, away from the others and in plain view. Everyone would see whoever sat at this table. I sighed.

"Here you are, honoured guest." The troll bowed again. I looked at the settings on the table, all labelled with neat little cards. I walked around the table. Then, I came face to face with the troll and frowned.

"Where are the spots for Yolanda and Katrina?" I asked. Neja had a spot right next to me—with Eddie on the other side—but I hadn't found any cards for my assistant or her sister. The guide looked nonplussed.

"Ah, they have been seated over there." The troll nodded towards the fireplace to the right, farthest from the doors. There was a table situated just outside the brightest light of the flames, looking very cosy and away from the line of sight. It was the table I wanted to sit at.

I rounded on Yolanda. "You have to switch with me."

"Uh…" She blinked her large eyes at me and looked just as confused as the guide.

"Honoured guest—" the guide started, a hitch in his voice.

"Pleeeaaassseee?" I begged. "You can sit with Neja, or if everybody wants to swap, then you and Katrina can sit here and Neja and I will sit over there. Or—oh, I have a better idea! We'll switch spots with two others at that table and we all can sit by the fire."

Now, had I been myself—that is, acting as I would have done otherwise—I would have asked around, found out who was sitting at the table, and wheedled an exchange through sheer politeness and as many smiles as I could muster. That was simply good marketing, getting what you wanted while the other person thought they were at the advantage. However, I was currently doing my best to annoy Eddie as much as possible, so I merely plucked up my name card and Neja's card and strode to the desired table, picking two names at random and switching them out, and hoping they didn't mind the sudden "upgrade."

The guide squawked and spluttered, but could not actively contradict me without going against whatever orders had been given by Eddie or offending me. This was how, some twenty minutes later when Eddie actually arrived in his tailored suit adorned with various medals and ribbons, he found himself sitting next to a pair of drow who looked thrilled to be so elevated, their backs straight and their expressions openly cheerful. Whereas I was seated next to my entourage, a young selkie woman wearing her sealskin as a shawl, a being of indeterminate gender covered in feathers, and a pair of brownies who were more than happy to discuss coffee with me.

"No, no," the elder brownie said, thwacking her younger companion on the arm. "You have to roast the beans over *low* heat to get the best result. A long, slow roast, none of this medium-low nonsense!"

"Yes, but if you do a medium-low heat on a rotating—"

"Enough!" Neja put her hands on the table with enough force to wobble the glasses, though none of them spilled. She eyed the two brownies and me with narrowed eyes. "Enough talk about coffee. Please. Talk about something else."

The younger brownie looked terrified, as though Neja had personally threatened him. The elder just nodded and took a sip of her glass of wine. The feathered creature tilted its head at me, opened its beak, then shook its head. The selkie carefully drank her water, the ice cubes clinking in place. Yolanda was peering over her shoulder to see if she could spot Boulder—I think he had been placed on the other side of the hall—and I couldn't think of any relevant topics of conversation that would not turn back to our plan of a coup, or coffee.

Katrina, thank goodness, came to the rescue. "So, tell me, who here has ever eaten roasted rock mouse? It's a specialty of our chefs, and I cannot tell you how difficult it is to catch those little monsters. They're so quick, you have to sneak up on them almost before you see them."

"Before...?" the feathered creature asked, voice breathy.

Katrina nodded eagerly. "There's this story about a troll boy who went out to play one morning. He was throwing rocks about—as young boys often do—and managed to kill a rock mouse. He was so pleased with this endeavour that he went out every day, randomly throwing rocks, and every day, he brought home a rock mouse. He became so renowned for his hunting skills that they trained him as a hunter. Only...he couldn't hunt a thing! Every time he tried to hit something, or snare something, he missed. Every time. But when it was random, he would bring down anything."

"That sounds improbable," I said. "Unless he made a deal with Life? She would do something like that, just for fun."

Katrina took my interrupting in stride and merely shrugged. "I don't know. I *do* know that one day this troll went out to go hunting, or what passed for his brand of hunting. He picked up a bigger rock than he normally threw—apparently, it had beautiful stripes— and examined it for crystals. Finding none, he tossed it over his shoulder and killed a wild wyrm who had been terrorising the mountains for decades. Everyone was so astonished at this victory, they made him our first king. Unfortunately, his nickname was rather unimpressive: Rock. They called him Rock. King Rock, too, which is almost worse."

There was a beat, then the entire table except for

me burst out laughing. I turned the words over in my head, tried to smile at them, and finally turned to Neja. "I don't get it," I whispered.

She patted my arm. "Don't worry, Cal. It's funny."

I nodded and chuckled as best I could. Katrina snickered again.

"Sorry, Cal," she said, hand covering her mouth. "You just look so confused!"

I sighed and wondered when the food was going to be served. Then, I realised that everything around me had grown silent. The other nearby tables, the people at my table, everyone was still, staring at something to my left. I turned in my seat and found Eddie in all his regalia, looking tall and decidedly displeased.

"Mr. Thorpe," he said, voice low and stern. His eyes flashed to Katrina, and I knew then he was fully aware it was she who had made everyone laugh. "May I have a word?"

Oh, yes, this plan was working out quite nicely, indeed.

CHAPTER 9

Eddie was fully aware that we couldn't very well have a private conversation standing right in the middle of the banquet hall. When I stood and replaced my napkin on my chair, I could practically feel everyone's eyes on us. Sebastian huffed in annoyance but did nothing; in this instance, idle gossip was actually a good thing. People couldn't help but notice I was sitting at a table meant for those lesser beings who held very little power. They would likely be wondering whether Eddie had done it on purpose, or if there was some sort of mistake. Those few who had witnessed the change would probably soon be spreading their version of the story all around the banquet hall. I was the one who had snubbed Eddie, not the other way around.

After pushing in my chair, I gestured for Eddie to lead the way, doing my best to look serene while I did so.

"Smile less," Neja whispered. I glanced at her. "You look creepy, Cal. Smile less."

I complied.

Eddie chuckled as we walked. "It would seem that the djinn has you wrapped around her little finger. I wonder how she acquired a companion so powerful as you."

He held open a small door near the fireplace, revealing a hallway leading who knows where. At least it was well lit, almost harshly so after the firelight of the hall. I blinked rapidly to adjust my eyes.

"She dropped a piano on me," I said, answering his question. Eddie froze, then burst out laughing. He had his hands on his stomach and everything, and I was fairly certain that he was going to start crying at any moment. I didn't think it was *that* funny. At the time, I hadn't thought it was funny at all, given how much it hurt.

"No, really," Eddie said, drawing a finger under his eye. "How do you two know each other?"

"Really," I said. I shoved my hands into my pockets and shrugged. "She dropped a piano on me. It was meant for someone else, but I got in the way."

Eddie stilled. He studied me for a moment as if he expected me to laugh and tell him I was joking. I wasn't. He cleared his throat and smoothed down his suit jacket. Now we were going to get into the actual business of the evening.

"I was wondering, Mr. Thorpe, why it was you switched the cards around for dinner tonight," he said. He wasn't using the translation spell, so his words came out genuinely, but he did tug at the tie around his neck, then at the sleeves of his shirt and jacket. He really did not want to be talking about this. I wondered, then, why it was he hadn't just let it be and eaten with the drow. Or was complacency a sign of weakness?

"I like the fireplace better," I said. "And Yolanda and Katrina were already sitting there. The drow did not at all mind switching places with me. Do you not find them pleasant dinner companions? I've never eaten a meal with the drow before, but I imagine they are pleasant enough."

Eddie forced a smile, flashing those ultra-bright teeth. "They are perfectly pleasant, and beyond thrilled to have been moved from a table of no consequence to one with severe power. A power you do not seem to wish to acknowledge or enjoy."

I frowned and pulled off my glasses, holding them up to the light. A little smudged. Carefully, I pulled out my handkerchief and cleaned them before replacing them on my nose. I looked up at Eddie and frowned again. My voice was quiet when I said, "Are you implying that Yolanda—my assistant and friend—is of little consequence? That the brownies are of little consequence? The selkie? I do not believe any one of them would appreciate the description."

Always ready with an answer, Eddie smiled. I imagine it was meant to be reassuring. "Compared to you, my lord, the entire room is of little consequence."

My lord. That was a new one, at least when not spoken in abject fear. I was tempted to snort at the title.

I did not. It was useful to know precisely how Eddie thought of me. Sebastian opened an eye in question, asking whether I needed to show off a bit. I mentally shook my head. I was more interested in a battle of words right now than outright displays of power. Maybe words would get Eddie's demeanour to crack.

"Compared to you, also?" I asked, tilting my head. "Or are your ambitions greater than opening up some trade agreements?"

Eddie's jaw clenched and his eyes flashed. Oh, yes, I'd hit a nerve. "We rock trolls have uncountable wealth beneath our very feet, something that all of Elsewhere values. A trade agreement with us would be quite valuable. But you saw our song spells, no matter how you tried to play them off. You know full well how truly powerful we are with those at our disposal. A master of spell songs, as I soon will be, is more than qualified to be your equal, wouldn't you agree, *Cal*?"

I bared my teeth in a loose smile. "Your song spells are interesting, yes. You can control a great force of nature. But do you honestly think that they can command an equal power to a being who stands in the spaces between Life and Death, who commands the power of the crossroads, who holds the limn in one hand, and the firm choice in the other?"

Eddie's jaw clenched further, and I was curious whether he would damage those pretty teeth if he continued. "Do you not understand what a song spell is? It is a way to command the very essence of our reality. To call forth whatever action you want. Only the most dedicated and the strongest can even manage a short one. What we can do? Keeping a single song spell going for *generations*? It's proof that we—that *I*—command greater capability than even you can imagine."

Ah, yes. There was that cult leader personality shining through.

Sebastian growled. I agreed. I requested, silently and with as much politeness as I could muster, that just a little power shine through my eyes, showing him the endless voids that Death bore, and the impossible chaos that Life contained.

"You wish to know why I snubbed you at dinner?" I asked, keeping my tone calm and even. "You wish to know why I would prefer the company of Yolanda and Katrina and Neja to yourself? You are ambitious, yes. Very well, I make a living off of the ambitions of many who wish the world to acknowledge them more, to grow their influence. But when you are ambitious at the expense of others? When you take away their choice, be it through force or sweet words meant to deceive them, then I object."

Eddie laughed, though the sound was strained. "The expense of others? What are you—"

"I know full well why rock trolls are led by those with a lesser amount of battle magic, why you choose the physically weakest among you to lead. Because they must then think of a different way than forcing others to their will. Because they must avoid war and conquest and all the things that would destroy your people. You are not like that. You are a slave to your ambitions, Eddie, and you will bring your entire culture down with you." I leaned in and glared at him. He met my gaze and flinched back. Sebastian writhed with glee at his discomfort. I could see plainly the yellow nimbus around Eddie, and the desire to reach out and touch him, to take his life and end all of this, was mouthwatering. To feel the surge of his lifeforce running through me. It would be so simple.

Instead, I leaned back and let Sebastian send more power through me. "As I am a being in between, I will give you a choice. Abdicate. Step down. Retire. Whatever you wish to call it. Declare yourself unfit for the crown, for the leadership of your tribe. Give up your ambition and be pleased with the progress that has already been made: opening up your borders, starting trade agreements with the rest of Elsewhere, sharing your culture. Or," here I held up a finger. "Or, you can continue this folly and I will do everything in my considerable power to stand in your way."

My ultimatum presented, I pulled back my power and let Sebastian return to coiling up inside me. I folded my handkerchief and tucked it away in my pocket, then turned to head back to my dinner. Hopefully I hadn't missed the main course.

"If I cannot win you over as an ally," Eddie muttered, voice shaking, "then I will just have to be known as the king who killed a Reaper."

With that cheerful warning, he wrapped his hands around my throat. They were massive, all encompassing, and large enough to knock off my glasses. With a shake and a twist, my neck snapped. There was a flash of white, very brief this time given that my death was so swift, and I returned to find my body falling to the floor. I managed to catch my balance in time to not squish my glasses. I leaned over, picked them up, replaced them on my face and turned to find Eddie staring at me, horrified.

He'd gone ghostly pale, his greyish skin looking like a corpse in the harsh light. His eyes were wide and terrified. His jaw was open slightly and I could have sworn I saw his hands tremble. "Y-you—" he tried to speak.

"I cannot die, Eddie," I said evenly. "No matter how hard you try."

"I…I did not mean to…it was just…" he trailed off, no explanations available for his attempted murder. Really, what can you say? If you murder someone, you don't usually expect them to carry on talking.

I sighed through my nose. "I must say, I'm disappointed. You could have made this so much easier for yourself. Very well, you have made your choice. Good evening, Eddie. Enjoy your dinner."

I straightened my tie and left him there, spluttering and gasping desperations. If Eddie did not step down, or invoke a rule to get him dethroned before the end of the week, then I would simply have to kill him. The thought sank to my throat for a moment then hesitated before settling deep in the pit of my stomach. I would not normally consider myself a killer, but it was not the first time I had done so, nor did I doubt it to be the last. I was a Reaper, after all, and I'm fairly certain people didn't respect my power because I handed out candy on major holidays.

I hadn't wanted this job, but I was going to take it.

The table was remarkably cheerful upon my return. Yolanda had apparently been keeping everyone entertained with some of the more amusing exploits of our office, including the ever-increasing attempts to make Agravane look ridiculous in our marketing campaigns. I had dressed him as an Easter bunny in the spring, despite Elsewhere not having that particular tradition, and that campaign did spectacularly well, garnering our most sales yet. I think the pink bunny ears coupled with the scowl helped. He never did believe that I was being completely serious in my intentions to make advertisements that sold.

"Cal!" Katrina said, smiling broadly as I slipped back into my seat. "You're just in time. They've started serving the main course. It's going to be a shepherd's pie with Stilton cheese and root vegetables. I think Eddie was trying to pick something very English, since that's where you come from."

"Shepherd's pie?" I asked, slightly disappointed. I was hoping for some sort of fish dish, or a curry or something with a bit of extra pizzaz. Besides, no one could beat my mother's shepherd's pie, no matter how hard they tried. Still, the meal choices could have been much worse.

Being at a table of little importance, we were served near the end, though the servers were swift enough for the food to still be steaming when they brought it. We were asked if we wanted any drinks refilled and then left in peace.

The elder brownie looked around, then spoke up.

"You know, we appreciate what you did, in choosing to sit here."

I blinked, my fork and knife poised over the crust of my pie. "Oh?"

"You…you gave us status when we don't really have any. Not here, not in Elsewhere, not anywhere. We're just the servants, or the ones people tell funny stories about, or the ones that are killed first. In sitting here, you give us status."

I lowered my utensils to the table. "I don't care if you're brownies or goblins or dragons, if you're good people, you're good people. And you seem quite decent. I don't see that being a brownie, or a selkie, or a…I'm sorry, I don't actually know what you are," I said to the feathered creature.

"Oh, I'm a Gamayun. In the mortal realms, you would know me as having come from Russia," the bird said, voice trilling and light.

"Gamayun," I repeated, rolling the word about. "Yes, I do apologise for not knowing your species, but my knowledge of magical creatures is still rudimentary."

Yolanda chipped in, "He's taking a correspondence course, but has only just started."

I shrugged.

Neja reached over and grabbed my hand, preventing me from cutting open my pie. "Cal, what happened with Eddie?"

I didn't much see any need to keep secrets from the people at this table, so I answered truthfully. "He tried to compare his power over the song spells with my

Reaper abilities, got angry when I disagreed, refused to give up the throne, and snapped my neck."

There were astonished gasps from the table.

"Oh, don't worry," I said, waving my hand dismissively. "It didn't take. I can't die."

I don't think that statement helped.

"Eddie tried to kill you?" Katrina asked, her voice suddenly dark, brimming over with anger. Her eyes flashed, her spine straightened and she gripped the fork in her hand as though it were a deadly weapon. She looked downright dangerous, a feat given the number of dangerous beings in the room. "He broke guestright," she snarled. "By rights, he should be exiled immediately."

"It's his word against mine," I pointed out. "And I'm fine. Very difficult to prove when I'm fine. Not even a drop of blood on me."

Yolanda shook her head. "Does not matter. He broke guestright. You only have to say the word and he will be put on trial. Only..." she trailed off and hunched her shoulders, looking at the table.

"Only what?" I asked. None of the other people at the table seemed willing to speak, perhaps still absorbing the news that Eddie, the guy they were all here to see crowned, had tried to kill me. I wasn't sure if my potential death was the more shocking thing, or the breaking of guestright.

My guess was that the guestright was the more scandalous. They were rules meant to keep the denizens of Elsewhere from tearing each other's throats out on sight and breaking them was akin to suicide. Eddie may have made his final mistake as the potential ruler. I perked up a bit.

"Only," Katrina spoke up, looking imperious and just as furious as before. "A trial must be presided over by the ruler of the tribe."

"Ah." That was not great news, as the Great Northern Ridge Tribe was currently without a ruler. "And if there isn't one?"

Katrina winced. Shook her head. "Then it's put to a general vote. Cal, you'd have to convince the entire tribe that getting rid of Eddie would be in their best interest."

"Easy," I said. Silence met my statement. "It would be easy, wouldn't it?"

"You're openly associating with the former heir, who chose love over duty to the tribe, solidifying our fate to choose from the lesser candidates of the blood-line," Katrina answered, sparing a sympathetic glance at Yolanda, whose shoulders were hunched again.

"Cal," Neja warned. I did not let her get much farther.

"The whole reason I came to this coronation was so that I could prove—definitively and without question—that Yolanda is awesome and that a great mistake was made when your former king *threw her off a cliff.* Oh, and because Life made me. Now, I'm not looking to put Yolanda back on the throne, because I don't think she wants it, but this seems like an opportune time to do exactly what I came here to do and also maybe improve your people's future. Wouldn't you say?"

More silence, but it was a little more hopeful, with quiet smiles tugging at the corners of mouths. I nodded firmly. "Alright, so how do I accuse Eddie so we can get this trial thing started?"

Yolanda, of all people, told me, a gleam in her eye that was either pleasure at her cousin's downfall, or gratitude for me. Or just a trick of the light. "You just tell him, in front of witnesses."

"Oh, is that it? Should be easy enough." I stood, my chair scraping across the stone and making an awful racket. Every conversation in the hall stopped and every eye turned to me. I turned to Eddie. "Eddie Rochefort, I am accusing you of breaking guestright by attempting to kill me in the hallway just a few minutes ago."

The silence in the hall didn't last. All the whispers turned to normal conversation, which then turned into near shouts of shock and excitement, I met Eddie's gaze evenly. Then, I smiled, sat, and ate my shepherd's pie.

I was right; it wasn't as good as my mother's. It was good, though.

CHAPTER 10

I shan't regale you with the details of whispers, proclamations of outrage, even the throwing of bodies backwards in shock, but needless to say my announcement did not go over calmly. Having accused Eddie of breaking guestright in front of his guests as well as his people was akin to committing murder right in front of these people. Worse, even. Everyone—and I do mean everyone—except Eddie and myself got to the edges of the room as quickly as possible, leaving the two of us standing there, regarding each other.

I felt like the star in one of Yolanda and Agravane's favourite soap operas, and frankly it was a strange feeling. I was a little surprised that no one was pulling out phones to share on the social media of Elsewhere, but then again, this was a formal event and I doubted phones were strictly allowed at Elsewhere formal events. The social criteria probably hadn't been updated for several centuries, after all.

"How dare you," Eddie said through gritted teeth. His fists were clenched at his sides and he was looking very flushed. His eyes darted to the people around the room before settling on me again, rage dancing there with abandon.

"I state only the truth," I replied in my best disinterested voice. Unlike my smiles, I had cultivated that voice extremely well. "You wished to know why I snubbed you by sitting somewhere else than beside you. I explained my reasoning, you grew angry, tried to compare our two powers, I disagreed, and you snapped my neck."

"You're not dead, though," Eddie pointed out, as if that were such a profound flaw in my argument.

"No," I said. "I'm *not* dead, because I cannot die. That does not change the fact that you attempted my murder. You did not know I can't die. You assumed that breaking my neck would be the end of me, the end of Life's representative, Death's employee and a Grim Reaper. You assumed that killing me would garner you great renown and make questioning you impossible. So you killed me. Just because it did not take does not mean it did not happen. Therefore, you violated the central core of guestright and I demand answers."

"Lies," Eddie snarled. I could see the edges of his shape shimmering as his battle magic came to the forefront. He was moments away from breaking loose and reigning terror down upon me. Unfortunately, as grand as the banquet hall was, I doubted that a fully fledged warrior troll in the throes of battle magic would be kept from doing damage to the onlookers.

And that was unacceptable. "You smear my name and attempt to destroy my house," Eddie said. "*You* are the one violating guestright, Reaper!"

More gasps sounded from the edges of the room. I saw a few delighted smile as well, probably from people who revelled in this sort of scandal. Also from the Fae, but they hated me for entirely different reasons.

I tugged at my shirt sleeves, trying to buy time. I really had no idea what I was doing and hoped that someone would intervene.

"Enough!" Katrina was the one who spoke out, stepping into the middle of the room with her head held high, glaring between us. A queen indeed, to be bold enough to get between her cousin and myself. "We cannot determine the truth of such matters here and now. A Telling must be convened."

"Good," Eddie snapped. "I will preside—"

"You will do no such thing," Katrina growled, clenching her hands into fists. "You are not crowned King yet, cousin. The Telling will require *all* tribe members be present."

Eddie's mouth twisted and his form flickered even more. He was inches away from full on battle mode. The bystanders seemed to see this; they began edging away, their own magics flaring defensively. Eddie whipped his head around as the first group managed to exit the chamber. He must have realised he was losing them because he closed his eyes and forced deep, calming breaths. His form solidified. Barely.

"Tell the kitchens to deliver the rest of the courses

to each of the guest chambers," he said to one of the trolls remaining in the room. "I will personally send letters of apology to the attendees. The Reaper will be—"

Katrina took another step forward. "Trial protocol has been enacted. Guards, you will escort Eddie to his chambers and keep him there until this can be resolved. Do not heed his orders. And escort Mr. Thorpe and his guests to his chambers, also."

This was news. I turned to Yolanda who nodded, the picture of seriousness. "Listen to her, Cal."

If that was what it took, then I could do that. Eddie looked more upset, shrugging off the attentions of the guards and stalking from the banquet hall in a huff. I went a little more slowly, if only because I wasn't quite sure where I was going.

We made it back to the suite without much difficulty. The guards did not speak to us Yolanda or I at all, instead pointedly looking ahead as they walked. Katrina left us just before arriving with a promise that we would receive more information tomorrow. Neja went with her, determination crossing her features, and also just a little bit of glee at the situation. That just left Yolanda and I alone in the suite.

Oh, and Tempest.

Tempest had ripped open the wrapping on the blanket we were meant to present as the coronation present and had burrowed into the material, wings covering her face while she slept.

"Bad griffin!" Yolanda waved her hands at Tempest,

who lifted her head and let out a squawk. "That was not for you!"

"Let her have it," I said, dropping onto the couch and wondering if this would be an opportune time to groan my dismay. By the time I decided on an answer, the moment had passed so I just propped my feet on the coffee table instead. "Even if Eddie is crowned, I very much doubt he will want the blanket now. Not from me."

"He is a coward and an idiot. A bloodthirsty fool who cannot think how to build an empire on anything but war and death," Yolanda said firmly, plopping down beside me. She folded her arms and huffed. "He should never have called you away from the table. That was inappropriate and I should have known that he would do something stupid if he talked to you in private."

"It wasn't your fault," I said. "I went with him. I snubbed him by moving those cards. This was what we wanted, wasn't it?"

Yolanda sighed and nodded. "Yes. It was the only way. His violating guestright is just as bad as using battle magic. More complicated, though."

I nodded. Leaning my head back on the cushions, I stared at the ceiling. The carvings took up most of the expanse, but there was a stripe just over the lintels for each room that was entirely empty. It looked like natural stone that had been smoothed over and polished to a definite shine, but in the corner I saw a tiny carving of a griffin family. Some builder's idea of whimsy amidst the carvings of gruesome battle, I imagine.

"Did *I* violate guestright first?" I asked. "By trying to help you and Katrina depose him? He said that I did by smearing his name."

"No," Yolanda replied, almost before I finished the question. She twisted her fingers together. "Guestright was put in place ages ago. Some say by the dragons, some say by the Elderkin. The whole point wasn't to stop political scheming and the movements of empires and reigns. It was meant to stop direct harm from coming to guest and host while sharing a roof. It has evolved a little since its birth, but not much. Scheming isn't a violation. Speaking badly of a host is incredibly rude, but not a violating of guestright. Breaking your neck is."

That didn't actually make me feel any better.

"What happens next?"

Yolanda shrugged. "I haven't done this before. I know the protocols, but it's been years, and…"

I turned my head to look at her and she sighed. She looked almost as depressed as Katrina had when she thought I'd get mad at her for Tempest chewing on my ear. Like the world had fallen from beneath her feet and there was no one to catch her. This would be the time where I asked what was wrong, but I wasn't sure how to phrase the question without sounding offensive.

For example: Yolanda, you look like Death warmed over. Why are you depressed?

Or: You're not as cheerful as usual. Why?

See? Not the best comforting questions.

Even a simple, "Are you okay?" would probably sound bad coming from me at the moment, flat and depressing. It was better than nothing, I supposed. I opened my mouth to ask, but she got to the answers part of the evening without my even asking.

"I was going to find Boulder after the banquet. We were seated on opposite sides of the room, and he didn't even make eye contact with me. I don't even know if he knew I was there and not here in our rooms. Then, well, *you* happened and now I'm stuck in here and can't talk to him."

"Are you two doing okay?" I had forgotten about Yolanda and Boulder, about their relationship troubles and all that had preceded this event. Finding out that your declared mate was still alive after having been told she had thrown herself off a cliff from the shame her people heaped on her must have been quite the shock. I made a mental note to have a conversation with Boulder, see how he was doing with all of this. It's not everybody who can walk into the scheming, chaotic, not entirely logical situations that follow me around and still come out of it with a sense of sanity. Yolanda, Agravane and Neja appeared to be the exceptions. "He seemed fine earlier, happy even, wanting to be with you...?"

Yolanda pressed her hands to her eyes and groaned. "It's been years since we've seen each other. He thought I was *dead*, Cal. Relationships don't just bounce back from that."

I thought about Neja and myself and decided that Yolanda was probably right.

"But..." Yolanda bit her lip and groaned again, this time not entirely a sound of despair. "It was just like it used to be, today and yesterday. Like no time had passed. He was so easy to talk with, and there was that extra spark when we—"

"Okay!" I sat up straight and leapt from the couch. "Time for popcorn."

My assistant gaped after me as I fled to the kitchens. Just as I rounded the corner, I heard her burst out laughing. "You're so weird, Cal!" she called.

Good. Weird and laughing was better than nothing.

For the rest of the evening, I made sure that we were fully stocked on popcorn and coffee, as well as whatever the kitchens had sent along—some sort of dessert thing and a cheese board. I dug out my laptop and we watched Yolanda's favourite soap opera, making commentary on the characters' choices and also laughing that Agravane was going to have to catch up when we got back.

You know.

A normal evening.

Sometime around midnight, though, with one season of the soap opera down and another queuing up, the mood in the room changed again.

Tempest had curled up between Yolanda and myself, her head buried between her paws. My hand rested on her back and, despite being low on coffee, I felt actually relaxed. Sebastian was sleeping, or whatever it was that the Reaper abilities did when they weren't awake and aware. I was tempted to just sleep on the couch. Yolanda was fishing the last piece of popcorn out of the bowl. She swallowed it whole, then set aside the bowl.

"Tomorrow, you're going to be taken to the drome," she said, voice barely above a whisper, as if the walls might overhear. Given Eddie's dislike for me, I wouldn't put it past him, though it was probably incredibly rude or something.

"The drome?" It sounded ominous, and also like something out of a comic book.

"It's where we gather the tribe at the start of battles. Two warriors give in to the battle magic and beat the daylights out of each other, to whet our bloodlust. It's...we haven't been to war for two generations and our warriors still train there in the hopes that they'll get that chance in their lifetime." She gave me a sad look and a half-smile. "The spell song and our immense riches are only one side of the coin when it comes to rock trolls."

"Just like my love of coffee and superior marketing skills are only one side of my coin." I looked at my hand and flexed the fingers. You wouldn't think that I had taken life with just a touch, but I had. Mostly, it had been an accident, a miscalculation on Death's part when he lent me his powers while I was his proxy. But it was also inherent in my Reaper abilities. I had been prepared to kill Eddie. I hadn't even thought about guestright.

I suppose the two of us were not that different. Only, he wouldn't come back if I killed him.

"Cal." Yolanda reached for my hand and squeezed it, the limb dwarfed in her grip.

"Keep going," I instructed, though I didn't let go of her hand.

"You'll be questioned by our eldest, the oldest members of the tribe. Eddie, too. Providing proof will be impossible for either of you since you were alone, so you're going to have to convince them by words alone."

"Them," I parroted.

Yolanda nodded. "Everyone. The eldest will only be questioning you. The tribe decides your fate. Good thing you work in marketing, right?"

I wondered if I were meant to laugh at that. Instead, I asked. "What happens to me, or Eddie, if one of us loses the trial?"

"They won't throw you off a cliff," Yolanda said. She sighed. "Being so high in status, second to Life and Death, you'll have to pay a weregild and that would be considered acceptable recompense. No one wants to offend someone so powerful, let alone Life or Death. It's not exactly fair, but little in the world of Elsewhere is. As you well know."

I did know. I knew full well that the rules of Elsewhere favoured the powerful, and that allying yourself with one of those beings was one of the best ways to survive this place. It also helped you lose what little control over your life you had, but I wasn't going to call people out for trying to survive. I'd seen too much suffering to do that. Dagmar, a human servant to the Winter Court of the Fae had given her entire life to try and serve, to be noticed and treated as an equal. She'd almost died for it. If I lost this trial, I'd only have to pay a weregild, despite being truly considered at fault. I had no idea what a weregild was, but I assumed I could afford it by the way Yolanda talked. She hadn't answered my question fully, though. "And Eddie?"

"He'll be banished. Not thrown off a cliff, that was a special circumstance. But he'll have no access to any tribe resources, and no other tribe will take him in. He'll be alone."

I wondered if consigning someone to death, like they had with Yolanda, was the kinder option. At least it would be quick—if Death didn't hire you away, that is—and there was no uncertainty about your fate. With banishment, no resources, no friends, no chance of reconciliation, well it was not a fate I would want to share. I supposed he could go live well amongst the other races of Elsewhere, but it would be a difficult start. I almost pitied him.

And then I remembered what it was he wanted and whose lives he was willing to step on to achieve that goal.

"What about you and Katrina and Boulder and Neja?" I asked. I didn't want to stand in the trial alone, but I also didn't want to drag anyone else into this. I had started this. It was my fault. Yes, I was working for the benefit of Yolanda's people, but I was the one who should be facing consequences. That didn't mean I liked the idea of standing before a crowd without any idea of what I was doing. I was a marketing agent; I manipulated online advertisements, I schooled my clients in the best way to answer interview questions, I made them look as good as possible. I wasn't the one in the spotlight. That wasn't how this whole thing worked.

I guess I would have to be my own client, now.

Yolanda patted my hand again. Tempest buried her head into my thigh.

"I may be able to be with you, as a guide to the protocol, but probably not. Because of my exile, you know."

"Should I ask for Katrina? If I need help explaining the protocols?"

Yolanda shook her head. "Don't draw any more attention to her right now. That might prejudice people against her when we start her bid for the throne. No, you'll have to ask for a representative to assist you. They'll assign an elder, or someone of similar status and knowledge of the protocols."

"It's better than nothing, I suppose," I said.

"You can do this, Cal," Yolanda replied, her voice firm, her expression determined. There was not an ounce of doubt in her tone or the set of her shoulders. She truly believed that I could pull this off. Not because I was a Reaper, or because I was second to Life and Death, but because she believed in me. Cal Thorpe.

I smiled and closed my eyes, letting the sounds of the soap opera lull me to sleep.

CHAPTER 11

*M*orning came with a squawk from Tempest, a crick in my neck, and the realisation that I hadn't changed out of my suit the night before and the material was now wrinkled beyond belief. I adjusted my glasses, patted Tempest on the head, and shuffled my way to the kitchen. Someone —I suspected it was Katrina's doing—had provided a container of food for the tiny griffin, which she dived after as soon as I opened the lid. She tore at the scraps of meat with a fervour I wished never to see again, getting gobbets of the stuff in her feathers and fur. She hissed at Yolanda as my assistant wandered into the kitchen, then went back to tearing into her meal.

"I don't suppose you know how to teach griffins table manners?" I asked as I set the coffee pot to drip. Tempest tilted her head back and swallowed what looked like most of a fish skeleton whole. I decided on toast for breakfast. No meat involved.

"The larger breed is usually very neat," was Yolanda's helpful response. I'd have to look up videos online on how to train the miniature griffin when we got back from this particular adventure. Or I could set Agravane to the task. Just imagining the look on his face when he realised the enormity of the task cheered me up a bit. Sebastian rumbled in agreement.

Yolanda and I went through breakfast and coffee before discussing anything more than our thoughts on Tempest, or the soap opera from the night before, or whether Agravane was handling the office well in our absence. Then, as I put the plates away, I turned to Yolanda.

"So…" I started.

She looked at me with grim expectancy.

"Is there some sort of dress code for these trials, or should I just wear whatever's clean. Because between Tempest and the travelling through rocks, and last night's sleeping arrangement, I'm not sure what I have that will suffice."

Yolanda sighed in relief, her shoulders slumping. "You have a strange sense of the important," she said. I shrugged and tried not to complain that it seemed important to me. "Just wear whatever you have that will impress and intimidate."

That narrowed my options a bit. Not enough, but a bit.

Some half-hour later, after a shower and a Yolanda-approved suit and tie combination, I was greeted by a knock at the door. Two very solemn guards in full battle regalia of the Roman variety greeted me, bowing so that I saw the tops of their helmets. They even wore short bronze swords at their hips. I wondered whether escorting me to the drome was considered an honour or a form of punishment. They might not have posed a physical danger to me except in the form of pain, but I got the message loud and crystal clear. Behave, Cal.

Yolanda and I fell in line. Tempest screeched behind the closed door of our suite, but I didn't need the griffin punctuating my speech with her noise. So we four walked in silence through the cavern kingdom of the Great Northern Ridge Tribe.

The drome, as it turned out, was a good two miles away from the guest suites. I hadn't expected the walk and my feet were protesting by the time we reached the arch that lead into the battle-to-the-death arena. Patent leather Italian shoes are not meant for trekking in. Unfortunately, I'd had worse shoe situations, despite the mild discomfort. The cobblers of Elsewhere were well employed by me.

The walk was done in silence, with neither words nor glances exchanged between me, Yolanda, or the guards, though several times I wanted to complain about my shoes. I half expected people to be watching the march to trial, but the hallways were empty. A strange tingle went up my spine the farther we went, with Sebastian turning over inside me. This felt almost dangerous. I didn't like it.

Finally, we reached a patch of daylight in the hall-way, an arched doorway to the outside, carved with depictions of battle and violence that were almost crudely done compared to the ones in my suite. Cheerful.

I lifted my hand to shield my eyes against the harsh light of day, then stepped out into what felt very much like a movie set from a Roman film. The guards, Yolanda and myself walked into a vast pit of pounded dirt the colour of sand. Surrounding this battleground —for there really was no other word for it—were stone bleachers stretching high enough to cast long shadows on the dirt. In the bleachers sat what I assumed was basically the entire population of the Great Northern Ridge Tribe, as well as the other dignitaries present for the coronation, who were sequestered in the middle, just below a box which extended slightly over the crowd. There were other boxes just like it at the four corners of the drome, but only this one was occupied with three trolls who were bent and grizzled with time.

Yolanda reached out and squeezed my shoulder before being escorted to the stands where Katrina and Neja sat. Boulder was there, too, somehow separate from the other dignitaries. He took her hand as soon as she sat, bringing it to his lips and saying something. Judging by the expression on his face, it wasn't a pleasant greeting. Yolanda nodded, mouth stretched in a line, and fixed her eyes on me.

If there was any chatter by the spectators, it fell quiet as I walked out into the dirt, the guards at my side. I stopped near the centre, faced the box, and straightened my tie. The trolls and dignitaries did not smile at my appearance. I did not expect them to.

I had dressed in unrelieved black. My suit was expertly tailored, with a waistcoat and black chrome pocket watch and chain, black shirt, black tie, even a black pocket square. With the high collar and my usual lack of expression, even I thought I looked particularly severe. Yolanda had assured me that I was terrifying and powerful. It was a new sensation to me. I had never been anything but average before, with glasses, brown hair and a face that would never grace the covers of magazines except as a background image. I had always been ordinary. Intelligent, yes. Capable, most certainly. But ordinary.

Things had changed.

Now, I was powerful. Dangerous. And I dressed for the part.

Across from where I stood, I saw Eddie and his escort enter the arena. He was scowling, glaring at the two guards at his side, both shorter and less muscular than he was. He wore the same suit he had donned at the welcoming ceremony, which while custom, did not fit quite so well as one would hope. The shoulders bunched and the button strained across his chest, as if he were an inch away from losing control of his battle magic and splitting the seams entirely.

Not a great start to the morning, then. This day would likely not go well.

Eddie walked up to where I stood and stopped about ten feet away. He gave me a perfunctory nod, still scowling, and turned to the trolls in the box. I did the same.

"We gather," the female elder called, her voice rasping like a rock fall. She was comparatively short, her limbs still slightly muscular despite her age, and she leaned on a staff of twisted wood that looked like it might collapse at any moment. Her gaze was frank, unrelenting and direct.

"We gather." The entire drome repeated the phrase, except for those who were not of troll blood. It unsettled Sebastian even more, to the point where it opened both eyes. I hoped whatever guise that kept my power from being openly visible was still in place. I didn't need to scare the very people I was trying to convince of my honesty. Intimidate? Sure. But not actively scare.

"The accusation has been made against our future king that guestright has been broken." The female troll pointed imperiously to Eddie, then to me. "The accuser stands on our proving grounds, the Grim Reaper, representative of Life, and representative of Death. Do you understand what now must be done, Reaper?"

This was what Yolanda had warned me about. I inclined my head in a respectful bow and spoke, my words echoing throughout the stone bowl with ease. "Wise elder," I said, "I am yet learning of the peoples and places found within Elsewhere and do not know your customs regarding such matters. I request an... advocate to explain things to me so that I do not insult your people in my ignorance."

The elders exchanged glances and whispers, looking at me and at the people in the stands. Finally, the female spoke again, wrinkles forming at the corners of her eyes as she relayed their decision. "Very well. Matron Mirabelle, you will act as advocate for the Reaper."

A female rock troll sitting near the bottom of the stands stood. She was slightly taller than Yolanda, with the typical broad shoulders and squat neck of her kind. There was something indescribably sad about her expression, though. She was also one of the few trolls wearing a dress, as though she alone expected something other than violence and did not need to dress for battle. She walked down to the dirt with quiet dignity and approached with a measured pace. She did not cower under the collective stare of her people and any whispers did not bend her spine.

She stopped just before me and bowed low. She did not spare Eddie a second glance.

"Greetings, Reaper. I am Mirabelle Rochefort, favoured consort to the late king. I am well versed in the protocols of our courts and am well qualified to assist you." Her words were formal, her voice deep. And, for a brief instant, her gaze flickered to where my friends sat before she looked at me again.

I did some quick mental calculations and nearly choked. "You're Yolanda's mother," I squeaked.

Eddie grumbled something and sneered at Mirabelle. She ignored him with quiet dignity, which only seemed to annoy him further.

"I…have no daughter," she said, voice cracking slightly, but her eyes flickered again to where Yolanda sat. "Not anymore."

Ah, right. The exile thing. Yolanda wasn't a formal member of the tribe and couldn't be recognised by them. I nodded, though that understanding was mixed with annoyance. "Still, I accept your assistance willingly."

She nodded, mouth tight. "The trial will begin with

you describing what happened to the witnesses gathered here. You will provide evidence, if any, to the state of affairs. Eddie will then be allowed to give his rebuttal. Following this, a vote will be taken."

I shoved my glassed up my nose. "It sounds fairly straightforward. Is there anything I *shouldn't* do?"

Mirabelle looked me over. "Don't release your Reaper powers."

Sebastian hunkered down inside me and I tried not to wince. "I can do that."

Yolanda's mother—that was going to be a long conversation for a later time—gave a firm nod and turned to the elders. "I have given him the basic instructions. You may proceed."

The female troll huffed and turned to Eddie. "I trust that you are well versed in the protocol, Eddie?"

He grunted agreement. "I know the rules." He cast a sidelong look at me, lip curled, eyes crackling with barely contained battle magic. I wonder if anyone had given him the same warning to keep his power in check.

"Very well, then. Reaper, begin your tale." The female banged her fist on the edge of the box, the sound reverberating with a *crack* startling enough to send shivers up my spine. At least I didn't jump. That would have done absolutely nothing for my intimidating reputation.

I straightened my cuffs again and took a long look over the crowd, making sure that they were all watching. Then, without sparing a glance for Eddie, I spoke.

"Yestereve, I attended the banquet meant to mark

the first political manoeuvre of the future king of the Great Northern Ridge Tribe. I found that I was not seated near my assistant, and given that I had things to discuss with her—work never ends, you see—I switched my seat, and that of Neja the djinn's, with two drow at the table where my assistant sat. The drow did not mind, and the other occupants of the table were very pleasant conversationalists."

I took a breath, wondering how much detail to give. Should I provide names? Conversation excerpts? Less was probably better in this instance. I didn't need to announce to the whole tribe how I was trying to depose their future king in favour of his half-human cousin, nor did I think relaying some of the funny stories about their people's history was a good idea.

"Sometime during the apéritif, Eddie came and announced that he would like to speak to me. I agreed and followed him into a hallway just off the fireplace in the banquet hall. There, I was asked why I was attempting to undermine him, and whether I disliked him. I was doing no such thing, only sitting with my assistant. He wanted to form an alliance, as he saw his control of the song spell of your people as granting significant power over the future of Elsewhere. I have no such interests; my duties lie between Life and Death, not with the changing political schema of Else- where. I do know that the power of the song spell does not match either Life's nor Death's, and certainly not both of them together. I do not mean to be arrogant," I said with a bow of my head, "but my power is signifi- cant, and I have not yet seen its equal, except in those whom I serve. Eddie did not appear to like my answer, for as soon as I turned my back, he said that instead of allying himself with a Reaper to gain power, he would simply have to be known as the king who killed a Reaper. Then, he snapped my neck."

Outrage filled the air in the form of shouts and snarls. Many of these came from the dignitaries and delegates who had come to witness the future king ascend, as well as to secure their own political alliances and dalliances. I couldn't tell whether they were outraged at my statement of my own power, which I hadn't even seen in full, or the fact that Eddie attempted to kill me. I hoped it was the latter.

"He is not dead!" Eddie shouted, his deep chest allowing his voice to carry above the crowd. Silence fell, obvious questions contributing to the tension in the air.

I shrugged. "I cannot die, no matter the means of killing. A side effect of my condition. I can still feel pain, however. That does not change the fact that an attempt was made, that harm was done. This, I believe, violates guestright, to which I agreed with the massive amount of paperwork that asked my dietary preferences, among other contractual obligations. I believe the other attending parties received the same paperwork."

"They did," Mirabelle said in an undertone. Eddie cast her a furious glance.

"You can prove none of this!" he said, grinding his teeth together.

"Eduard, you speak out of turn!" one of the elders

said. Some of the other trolls were beginning to mutter to themselves, looking between myself and Eddie. The elders banged their fists on the box a few times and the noise died down.

The female elder looked down at me. "Reaper, what evidence can you provide for these accusations?"

"I have no witnesses to report," I said. "However, I can prove my inability to die, which will lend some veracity to my statement."

"Do so, then."

I looked around for a target to kill me. Eddie was out, for obvious reasons. I didn't want to go to the guards for fear that they would decide to stab me and ruin my very best intimidating suit. Mirabelle might do it, though, and it was probably better than Yolanda, who would likely be considered biased. Though, I had no doubt that Yolanda would be perfectly happy to kill me, just for fun.

I turned to Mirabelle. "If you would be so kind as to break my neck?"

She reared back in horror. "I cannot!"

"It will do no permanent damage, I swear it," I said, holding out my hands in supplication.

"I understand, Reaper, but I cannot do this. It would violate guestright." Mirabelle bowed low. I had thought the whole thing was moot given the trial, but apparently that was not the case. Politics was complicated.

"I'll do it." I turned and found Neja standing in her stadium seat, a ferocious grin on her face. She turned her head to the elders. "Is this acceptable to you?"

"Yes, djinn, it is." The elders leaned forwards, eagerness a little too apparent in their gazes. It was a little disconcerting to realise that the entire population in the seats was leaning forwards with bated breath to see me die, but then this was a species eager for battle and blood. At least, I didn't think I was *that* annoying. Perhaps my work over the last couple of days had been more effective than I thought.

"Try not to ruin my suit!" I called, just as Neja drew a knife from her belt. She sighed, a long-suffering sound.

"I'll do my best, Cal," she said, then threw the knife. It went straight for me and I had to fight every instinct to duck and run, instead keeping perfectly still. I expected the knife to go straight for my chest, but instead it went for my face. Before I could react to that change, the blade had pierced my left glasses lens and gone straight through my eye.

Neja had good aim. She hadn't ruined my suit.

She'd ruined my glasses, instead.

As usually happened when I died, everything went white. Sometimes my excursions to this bright, empty place lasted an instant, sometimes a few moments. This time, I was there long enough for something extremely strange to happen.

"Hello, Cal," someone greeted me. I spun around, trying to find the source of the voice. *My* voice.

"We need to talk."

CHAPTER 12

My reaction to meeting, well, myself was not particularly graceful. I gaped. And gawked. And finally squeaked out an incoherent demand to know what in the world was going on.

My double just blinked at me. He was me. I was him. We were wearing the same suit, bore the same glasses, even had that stupid flop of hair that wouldn't stay put no matter how much gel I used. The only differences were the expressions we bore. I was staring like a fish. (This is mere guesswork, given I had no mirror in this strange white place, but I could feel my jaw hanging and so surmised it to be an accurate description.) He looked bored.

The other difference, and this was a bit more serious, were his eyes. Mine were a pleasant and ordinary brown. His were black. Almost entirely black. The iris and sclera were completely black. It was almost like looking at the voids in the universe that were Death's eyes, but not quite. Because the pupils were yellow.

Bright, vivid yellow. The same yellow as the auras around people who were about to die that I saw when using my Reaper abilities.

"S-sebastian?" I asked, my voice wobbly. My double inclined his head.

"The one and the same."

"You look like me!" My exclamations were getting slightly more terrified, my voice pitching higher with each statement.

"We don't have time for this right now, Cal. Neja is going to pull the knife from your eye at any moment, and then you'll come back to life. We need to talk *now*." Sebastian clenched his fist and snarled, sounding so much like the eldritch being inside me that I immediately nodded my head and took a deep breath.

"Okay. Talk."

"You're becoming unstable, Cal. I was created through an interaction between Life and Death when your Reaper abilities came to life during the period you were acting as Death's proxy. I'm not *supposed* to be a separate being to you, but there's nothing to bridge the empty gap between you and me. I take over sometimes, but that's it. I can't support you for much longer. Nor can you support me."

I shook my head. "I don't understand. What do you mean, *support* me?"

Sebastian reached out and grabbed my arm, holding up my hand so I was forced to stare at it. The fingers were ever so slightly transparent. I started gaping again.

"You're fading, Cal! You may not be able to die

without a soul, but you can't exist like this indefinitely. Certainly not with this much power flowing through you. We ought to be one entity, not three!"

I considered myself a relatively intelligent person, but whatever it was that Sebastian was trying to get across short circuited at the realisation that my fingers were fading away. "I'm disappearing!" I squeaked. I flapped my fingers through the air, as though that might dispel the fading.

My double reached out and grabbed the lapels of my jacket, bringing me in close so I could stare into the strange eyes and furious expression he bore. If this was what people saw when my Reaper abilities came into effect, then I understood why they were frightened. "Yes, Cal. You're disappearing. Your emotional quirks are only the start. Soon, you'll be nothing but an empty shell. Life and Death will have to order you to do your job. Remember that feeling just after Al Capone escaped your body? When you could do nothing but think logically and had no emotions? It'll be worse, Cal. You won't have a singular, independent thought, logical or otherwise at all."

"What do I—we—do?!"

Sebastian put me down. As soon as he did, the whiteness of the empty plane started to fade, replaced with colours vaguely similar to the drome. I heard three words before I blinked my way back to life.

"Find our soul!"

As if things weren't complicated enough for me right now.

I blinked a few more times and the world resolved

itself around me. Neja was leaning over me with a wide grin. "Welcome back, Cal," she said.

"Ugh," I replied. Everything was slightly blurry. I rubbed my eyes and found that my left cheek was smeared with blood and other gore. "Eeww," I said, shaking my hand in disgust. "There are cleaner ways to kill a person!"

Neja helped me stand. Mirabelle, who was hovering nearby with wide eyes, hastily reached into a pocket and pulled out a handkerchief. I muttered my thanks and scrubbed my face until Neja gave me a nod of approval. Then, she handed me back my ruined glasses. The left lens was completely missing, but the right one was still whole and miraculously unscratched. At least I could see a little bit.

"At least I didn't mess up your suit," Neja said. Then, she turned me by my shoulders so I was facing the elders again. They—and the rest of the audience—were staring at me with varying degrees of alarm. Neja patted me on the back and went back to her seat, looking a little smug.

Finally, the female troll that was leading proceedings spoke, mouth twisted in disgust. "The, ah, point has been proven…Thank you, sir Reaper. I, ah, that is… Eddie, you may now speak."

Frankly, I had forgotten about Eddie. Meeting myself as Sebastian was occupying a great deal of my mind at the moment and I really wanted to drag Neja and Yolanda away to demand an explanation. Or summon Death, for much the same reason. I figured Life would just laugh at my situation and send me on my way and so didn't count her in my calculations. For crying out loud, I didn't even know where to *start* looking for my soul. This could be very, very bad.

Eddie was fuming, fists clenched at his sides and whole body trembling. He was barely in control right now; anything could set him off and I didn't like the chances of those innocent bystanders if he gave in to the battle magic.

"Perhaps you should take your seat," I told Mirabelle. Yolanda's mother looked at Eddie, then at me, then at her daughter. She winced and nodded, walking back to her seat with the same dignity that she'd worn in leaving it. If anyone was going to stand between Eddie and destruction, it would be me. Fading or no fading.

The angry rock troll took several deep breaths and some of the trembling seemed to subside. He tugged at his suit jacket, which was still ill fitting, and addressed his audience. The personable cult leader facade was cracking slightly, but Eddie still bore a great deal of charm.

"Friends," he said with a low, sweeping bow. "I have been honoured to celebrate this week with you. My coronation means nothing if I cannot celebrate with those that mean so much to me. My people. Our people. It was with this mindset that I invited everyone to attend my coronation, and with joy that I accepted the Reaper's presence here. How better to show the world the wonders of the Great Northern Ridge Tribe than to have so illustrious a guest here at my humble coronation?"

He swept his hand towards me and I resisted the urge to snort. Then, Eddie turned back to the audience, his hands once more clenched into fists.

"The first insult came almost immediately. The Reaper brought his assistant with him, specifically to undermine the new age of our people. For who else is his assistant but Yolanda Rochefort, our former heir to the throne! Banished for abandoning her people and choosing an outsider as her mate."

Eddie pointed at Yolanda, who lifted her chin and made no move to flee, despite the sudden roaring of the crowd. There were shouts about how she should be dead, how she shouldn't be among them. How she abandoned them.

Yolanda's eyes were wide, her expression slowly turning to dismay as the shouting grew louder. The invited guests to this whole event watched with bated breath, as though this were a sporting match or a popular television show. Then, there was movement.

Boulder stood. He clasped Yolanda's hand in his own and turned to glare at the crowds in the stands. Silence fell over the arena, as shocked by his standing as by his glare.

"How *dare* you!" Boulder snarled, the sound like the tumbling of rocks and just as loud. Whatever earth magic he possessed was amplifying his voice enough so that everyone felt his words. I felt them as a vibration in my bones, enough to make me clench my teeth. "You *dare* shout such obscenities at the person who cared *everything* about you that she would give up our love for you?!"

Yolanda flinched.

"Give up her love?" Eddie scoffed. "She—"

"Was thrown off of a cliff by her own father!" Boulder was seething, his eyes flashing. The stands around him began to tremble, the rock reacting to his emotion. I knew that he was a mountain nymph, a creature attuned to the rock and stone and earth, but this was more than I ever expected of the guy. I liked him even more, now.

There were murmurs again in the crowd, the trolls whispering to one another as though Boulder's statement was news. Mirabelle, sitting only a few seats away from her daughter, closed her eyes and clenched her jaw.

Boulder scoffed. "Oh, you did not know?" he asked, tone mocking. "You think that the person who had trained her whole life to take the throne, who spent countless hours among you, talking with you, learning about you, seeing to your needs, just disappeared one day because she didn't want the job? No! Her father—your *king*—threw her off a cliff without trial or explanation and she only lives now because Death saved her. She and I loved each other with the strength of the mountains, and yet after her own father rejected her for loving one not her own, she did not come find me. She did not seek to live amongst my people—who would have welcomed her gladly—because she could not stay with her people. Instead, she worked for Death. For his Reaper. Alone."

The murmurs were stronger, now. Boulder nodded firmly. He pointed to Eddie. "He knows the truth. He knows the truth of what happened. He knew even before the Reaper arrived that Yolanda was going to be here and so invited me to sow discord. Fine. But none of this, not one piece of this, has *anything* to do with Eddie's violation of guestright!"

The last word echoed through the drome, an accusation so pointed that Eddie rocked back slightly on his feet. He glared at Boulder and Yolanda before wiping the expression from his face and replacing it with a gentle smile. He spread his hands in supplication.

"I never said it did. I was only providing some context for the whole situation," Eddie said, still smiling. The trolls shifted in their seats, and even the dignitaries were looking impatient.

The female elder slapped her hand on the stone balcony again, calling the unruly audience to attention. Eddie turned to her, his expression as polite as he could make it. She spoke, voice rasping. "We want no context, Eduard. We want only the events of yestereve."

Eddie nodded and ground his teeth. He tucked his hands behind his back. "I indeed asked the Reaper to speak with me in the hallway regarding a potential alliance. It did not seem to me to be something one discussed in front of...certain parties."

Yolanda huffed loud enough for the entire drome to hear, making sure everyone knew what parties those were. The brownies and selkie stiffened as well, eyes bright with indignation.

"We stepped into the hallway and I mentioned the possibility of an alliance between our peoples, as equals, which was soundly rejected. I then let the

Reaper return to the table. Before I could even get back to my meal, I was accused of violating guestright. That is all, elders."

Eddie spoke smoothly, ending his statement with a bow. It would have been a well-done speech except for two things. One: he made Boulder angry, and Boulder was a far more passionate speaker than Eddie, for all his charm. Two: every time he looked at me, he started trembling again, barely in control of the fury that triggered his battle magic, the sign of anything but quiet acceptance of my rejection to his alliance.

The elder raised her hands for attention, though everyone was already watching her. "We have heard the stories. Now it is time to deliberate. Everyone return to their work. We will take the vote tomorrow."

The guards who had led me to the drome now approached again, prepared to fetch me away from it. They were eyeing me speculatively, looking at my glasses and at Yolanda and Boulder, still sitting in the stands. Neja strode towards me, as unconcerned by the events as ever. She linked arms with me.

"So about your glasses," she said, wincing up at the frames. "Did you pack a spare pair?"

"No." I was tempted to grumble, but it wasn't worth it. "But I have more back at the office. Yolanda is smart enough to order in multiples."

"Good." Neja nodded firmly.

We went back to the suite, where Tempest was flying about in obvious agitation. She screeched at our entrance and dived towards the guards. They raised their arms and ducked their heads, but the tiny griffin turned on her tail and landed on my head instead, muttering her annoyance and being cooped up. I reached up and patted her absently.

"I know I'm not supposed to interact with people so I don't influence anyone unduly, but if we could arrange an escort to the outside so Tempest could fly about, that would be greatly appreciated," I said in the general direction of the guards. They said nothing, only exchanged a glance with each other, then left. The door shut ominously behind them.

I collapsed on the couch, dislodging Tempest from my head, and let out a groan. "My feet hurt. Why does the drome have to be so far away from the guest suites?"

"To avoid unnecessary bloodshed," Neja said, as if it were the most obvious thing in the world. I grunted. She sat next to me, much more delicately, like a cat curling up with pointed claws tucked beneath itself. I really hoped Neja cleaned the knife she had killed me with. I didn't need more gore around.

"So," she said, reaching out to straighten my hair. "That went well, don't you think?"

"I met Sebastian." I rolled my head on the back of the couch to look at her. She merely furrowed her brow.

"You always have Sebastian inside you. I don't think this is new."

"When you killed me. I met Sebastian. Talked with him. He looked like me, except for his eyes, which were black and yellow." I gestured vaguely to my own eyes. Neja frowned, her brows furrowing deeper. "He said that we have to find my soul soon, or I'm going to disappear. Apparently, I'm not meant to be split into thirds."

I held up my fingers and waggled them, almost expecting to see them fading away as they had in that empty place. Neja went absolutely still, not even a breath passing her lips. Then, she sagged.

"Oh, stars. You're destabilising, aren't you?" she asked.

I shrugged. Waggled my fingers again.

"Destabilisation is when a being not born with magic gains magic—it's more common than you think —but the power can't take proper hold for whatever reason. Sometimes the being isn't meant to have power, or it's the wrong kind of power, or something else. As a djinn, I've seen it a lot. You'd be surprised how many people wish for magic and power. It doesn't always work, for various reasons."

"Like not having a soul to keep everything in one piece?" I asked. My voice was darker than I had intended it and I immediately snapped my mouth shut. I didn't need to spout more dark theories about the mess I was in. I had enough problems without giving Life more ideas.

Neja brushed her hand across my cheek, the touch warm. It was probably meant to comfort me, but all I felt was the warmth of her skin. "Humans are tricky creatures. They're always born without magic, but can acquire it relatively easily. It doesn't always end well."

"What will happen to me?" I asked. Neja pulled her hand away.

"The power will consume you until you are nothing more than a vessel for it. It, in turn, will lose its ability to affect the world, instead just existing inside an empty shell with no will, no drive, no movement. In effect, you will be comatose. Forever, since you can't die."

Great. Just what I needed.

"How long will it take?" I could barely form the words and I realised that I was actually afraid. Truly, deeply afraid.

"It can take years. Or months. If Sebastian has contacted you, I'd say months is more accurate. Death would know better."

I took off the remains of my glasses and pressed my hands to my eyes. It was Death's fault that I was in this situation in the first place. I knew it was an accident, but that didn't change the fact that this had been *done* to me. Well, I would simply demand he help me fix it. If he could.

"Don't tell Yolanda, okay?" I asked. "Or Agravane. Just…not for a while. Not until we have to. I don't want them to worry."

Neja leaned into me and I lowered my hands from my eyes to look at her. Her eyes were soft and her mouth thin, but there was gentleness in her mien. She lay her head on my chest and twined her fingers with mine. It was the most intimate contact we'd ever shared, including that kiss the other night. My heart beat faster.

"Whatever you want, Cal," she breathed.

That would have been the perfect moment to say

something romantic, or at least honest and open since I wasn't very good at the whole romance thing, but the dratted griffin let out an earsplitting shriek just as the door burst open and Katrina ran inside, breathing hard.

"Eddie's vanished!" she said. I blinked at her, not comprehending why she was panicking. "With the scrolls where the song spells are written!"

Okay, now I understood the panic.

CHAPTER 13

You would think that Eddie running off with the lifeblood of the tribe would have automatically granted me a victory in the trial, endearing me to the people of the tribe and casting Eddie as the villain. However, thanks to some legal loophole set up generations ago, any crime committed by a tribe member while on trial did not influence the outcome of that trial. Katrina said that it had come about when some elder was on trial for food theft, and then proceeded to rob the jewel vault blind. They'd had to complete the trial about food theft before they could even begin to unravel the jewel vault robbery. Apparently stealing food was—at the time— more of a crime than the other, jewels being so common and all. Katrina didn't know whether that was still the case.

The fact that Katrina could talk so swiftly while also running was quite impressive. Frightening, but impressive.

"If I haven't won the trial—which I should have, because his fleeing is obviously a sign of guilt—then where are we going?" I asked, running along beside her as best I could manage. Oddly enough, all this time as Death's marketing agent had made me a proficient runner. I didn't really want to think about the reasons for that, instead preferring to think that my flight response was well honed, and focused on not tripping over pebbles instead. Tempest shrieked encouragement as she flew beside me, having followed us from the suite.

Neja, who was leading the procession despite not knowing where we were going, turned her head long enough to shout at me. "To find Eddie, obviously!"

"I am not a scent hound," I retorted. I had no idea where Eddie had gone. I got lost from the suite to the banquet hall, so could not possibly compete with someone who had grown up in these tunnels. It was a labyrinth combined with a maze combined with a rubik's cube. Impossible. "I do marketing!"

Katrina directed Neja through a low corridor, the ceiling barely tall enough for me, which must have made it an absolute horror for most rock trolls. It was likely a shortcut cultivated by the children, but it served us well because we burst into the main hall a few moments later. Neja slowed herself to a capable walk and Katrina immediately stopped, hugging the walls to avoid undue scrutiny. I am neither that graceful nor that aware, so I stumbled directly into a group of trolls. Tempest chirruped and landed on my shoulders.

"Apologies," I said, straightening and brushing off my suit. "I wore the wrong shoes for running."

Mirabelle appeared out of nowhere and put her hand on my back, gently guiding me to where Katrina and Neja stood. She looked alarmed, her eyes wide and her breath a little shallow. "You came."

"I did," I said. "Though I don't know how much help I can be."

"It's not you," Katrina said, too quickly for politeness. "We need Tempest."

I looked at the owl-faced cat with wings on my shoulder and blinked. "Um…?" was about the most coherent thought I could manage. "Go for it?"

"Griffins are excellent trackers," Mirabelle whispered, looking about to see if anyone was listening to us. They were all occupied with their own conversational groups and hardly paid us any attention, despite my supposed status. It felt almost normal, which was nice, until I remembered what was going on. I tugged on my collar. "We breed the small ones as guardians and trackers. They will follow their handler's instructions to the ends of Elsewhere, and Tempest is our best."

"She means that we need you to direct Tempest because she won't listen to anyone else anymore," Katrina said. She was looking more distraught by the minute, wringing her hands and shifting her weight back and forth. Mirabelle also looked suitably grim. "This is so bad. Who is going to lead us now? Where's Yolanda?"

"Probably with Boulder," I said, though I did look

around the room to see if I could spot her. In fact, I saw none of the other dignitaries invited to the coronation. Only trolls, and not even the full population at that. The trolls in the room were either of similar age to the elders or Mirabelle, likely the most level-headed of the entire group. At least someone was showing some sense, though they all just seemed to be standing around, doing nothing but talking.

Mirabelle gave a sigh as she finished examining the crowd, and if I didn't know better, I would have said it was one of relief. "The others have been asked to remain in their quarters. Yolanda will be safe with Boulder."

Katrina let out a sound that was somewhere between a whine and a squeak. "But that means we don't have anyone of the bloodline left to—"

"We have you," Neja said, slinging an arm around Katrina's waist and smiling fiercely. Katrina yelped.

"Indeed," I said, scratching Tempest's chin while studying Katrina. She seemed to shrink even more. "That is what we were trying to do, after all. Get Eddie out of the way so that you could take the throne and keep your people from going to war. Granted, these are hardly the circumstances I had envisioned, but *someone* must step up, and you are the only one who can."

Katrina's shoulders rose up to her ears and she flushed a burnt orange. "I...didn't think you were serious," she breathed. "I mean, Yolanda is obviously—"

"Yolanda gave up her position," I said firmly. "She could have returned after Death hired her. She could have easily staked her birthright and had Eddie thrown out on his heel before any of this. She didn't want it. *Doesn't* want it. She gave it up, and frankly, I think you're the better option. You have a firm grasp of political and economic spheres, remember?"

Katrina's mouth hinged open and closed a few times while she digested my words. In the end, she nodded once. Twice. "Okay." She took a deep breath. Her shoulders straightened. Her chin rose. "Okay."

Neja turned Katrina by the shoulders and gave her a shove towards the front of the hall. Mirabelle shot me a grateful look and followed, her broad shoulders pushing her way through the crowd in a way that Katrina, being half-human, couldn't. Eventually, the pair made it to the raised dais and Katrina climbed up, facing the crowd.

"I am Katrina Rochefort, last daughter of our late king, heir to the throne," she said in a firm voice. I nodded and felt the barest hint of a smile on my face. Sebastian let out a low hum of approval. "You all know what has happened with Eddie—"

"Thief!" a voice cried out.

"He stole our spells!" another called.

Katrina held up her hands for silence, and despite being tiny compared to her people, and having not a single stich of battle magic, everyone fell quiet and watched her with rapt attention. I had never seen a society that followed its physically weakest member as its leader, but it was absolutely fascinating.

"I know that Eddie has wronged us, but we can do nothing about it until we *catch* him. Now, I have the Reaper here with his griffin, Tempest. He has graciously offered her to us to help in our pursuit of Eddie. However, I need something of Eddie's to follow." Katrina looked out over her audience. There were mutterings and questions thrown back and forth. "His blood would be best, but as that is not readily available, I would be happy with some clothing or a shoe."

One of the guards that had been at the trial earlier stepped forwards, something large and fabric grasped in his fist. "Eddie left his suit jacket with me before he, ah, disappeared," the guard said. I assumed that meant before Eddie had bamboozled him and given him the slip.

"That will work very well, thank you." Katrina bestowed a glowing smile on the guard, who blushed, then turned to me. "Please, Reaper, if you will. We have not a great deal of time."

The guard practically ran the suit jacket over to me and retreated just as quickly once I had taken it. It was truly massive, but I held it up to the comparatively minuscule Tempest anyways. "Okay, girl. I assume you know how to do this, so I'll just say that if you find Eddie, then I'll make sure you get a whole fresh fish for a month. Promise."

Tempest perked up, giving me a serious look, then let out a cry that filled the entire cavern. With two beats of her wings, she was airborne and surging through the air towards the back of the room. I stood dumbstruck, holding the suit jacket. Neja elbowed me in the side and I yelped.

"Follow her, genius."

"Oh." I ran after the griffin.

Now, it will probably surprise no one to know I grew up without a cat or dog. My mother was very fond of animals, but decided that a child me was not the best combination with a dog whom I was liable to get into trouble. She also didn't think that a cat would have survived peacefully in our household. I think it had something to do with Baz, who was running wild through our house several times a week, but that's besides the point. I did, though, have fish.

Fish do not run.

Or fly.

Let me say, therefore, that following a griffin through the multitudes of caverns that made up the Great Northern Ridge Tribe kingdom was a new experience. Tempest moved faster than I had expected, every wingbeat of hers taking me three steps to catch up. I might have had some practice in running, but chasing after a flying cat monster?

Nothing prepares you for that. Not even running for your life, though it is very good for cardio.

"Tempest!" I called, ducking through an archway that led to another intersection. I swear, they needed street signs to tell you where to go. Instead, there were carvings. Everywhere.

I had lost sight of Tempest, which was bad. I heard a scree from the left corridor and followed after. "Can you fly slower?" I huffed, though I doubted that she would listen. Indeed, for my trouble, I got scolded with a series of annoyed chirps as she winged onwards.

Maybe this was why my mother had never bothered with pets. The insubordination.

After what felt like many, many hours of running, at which point my legs were entirely jelly, Tempest came to a point where she could not pass. It was what appeared to be a solid wall, the carvings there thicker and darker, depicting a battle scene wherein many of the participants had their innards strewn about. I couldn't tell which side was winning, but it didn't matter. Tempest was flying back and forth in front of this wall, muttering angrily. Every now and again, she would dive for a particularly vivid carving of a troll standing on the head of its enemy, but the wall was solid and she was brought up short.

I arrived, panting and wheezing, and Tempest proceeded to scold me, her tail lashing. She landed on my shoulder, sides heaving and wings flaring.

"She wants to go through the wall."

I yelped and jumped, turning to face Neja followed by Katrina, both hardly out of breath. "Have you been following me the whole time?" I demanded.

"Of course," Katrina said. "I have to keep an eye on you until the trial is over."

"I just thought you might need help," was Neja's less than helpful reply. I narrowed my eyes at her and she shrugged. Tempest let out another cry and dived at the wall, scratching it with her talons before returning to my shoulder.

"She wants to go through the wall," Katrina said again.

"Maybe she got the scent wrong." It seemed unlikely

that she could possibly have followed Eddie's scent through a wall of solid rock, but what did I know. "It's a dead end."

"This is an old part of the complex." Katrina ran her fingers over the carvings. "I haven't seen carvings like these in ages. I thought they were all forgotten or reworked. Even for a battle-hungry race like rock trolls, we don't usually go for art that's this violent."

"Cheerful," I said, because it seemed like the sort of thing that you say when desperately trying to catch your breath and someone is discussing art. Neja patted my arm in silent support of my breathing efforts.

Katrina, though, was bent over the carvings, peering at every line and whorl, every bloody scene and violent detail. She ran her fingers over the stone like a caress. Frankly, it was a little creepy. Then, with a bit of pressure on the eye of the skull under the troll's foot, the entire wall cracked open. A panel slid back, revealing a darkened corridor like this was some sort of movie and secret passages were normal.

Neja immediately drew a knife, sliding her feet into a defensive stance. Katrina jumped to the side and peered into the darkness. Tempest let out a cry of triumph and dived forwards, her wings beating at the air as she followed her quarry.

I stood there. Again.

"Cal," Neja prompted. "Go on."

"Why do I have to go first?" I complained.

"Because you can't die, remember?" Neja prodded me in the ribs. I sighed the sigh of the long suffering,

Sebastian echoing my sentiment, and started running again.

Of course, as soon as I entered the dark and creepy tunnel, the ambient light of the caverns practically vanished. My eyes adjusted to the darkness faster than I expected. There was some sort of light up ahead that let me see enough to not trip over any stray rocks, which was good because there were a lot of stray rocks. The other corridors and tunnels were all immaculate, but this one was a mess, like it had been forgotten on purpose.

Figures that Eddie knew of a forgotten tunnel in this place. For once in my life, I'd like to stop following people into forests or disused tunnels or the middle of Renaissance parties (okay, that was just that once). My shoes really couldn't handle this sort of abuse.

Tempest let out another cry, this one sharper, and I ran faster. There were other noises besides her triumphant screeches, and I recognised them as heavy footsteps and angry curses. Someone was running. We'd found Eddie.

The passageway opened up suddenly, emptying into a vast cavern with some sort of underground river running through it. The light brightened and I realised that this whole place was well lit, likely because it had docks with an armada's worth of wooden boats, all looking in good repair, if absolutely ancient. Most of them were dry docked, but one was in the water, waiting for its captain.

Eddie was trying to make his escape on this forgotten armada, already halfway to the boat, but

Tempest dived at him, buffeting him with her wings and claws before flying up and around to do it all over again. Eddie waved his arms furiously, trying to beat her off. In one hand was a scroll that fairly hummed with magic and it was this that I assumed everyone wanted back.

My stumbling must have caught Eddie's attention, because he whirled on me and let out a furious snarl. "You think you've won?" he demanded.

"Um," I replied, still catching my breath.

Then, Katrina and Neja appeared, both honing in on Eddie like Tempest had done. Neja drew her knife and Katrina let out a cry of fury. "You have stolen our most sacred spells! Return them and face the justice you deserve!"

Eddie sneered, still backing towards the boat. Tempest had retreated slightly, circling above him. If he took two more steps, he would be at the boat. If he untied the rope, the river's current—swift, angry— would take him out of our reach before we could do much more than protest.

"Justice? From *you,* a half-breed with no magic to speak of? You'll never be the leader I was going to be! You will never lead our people to glory!" Eddie laughed in Katrina's face, his features turned ugly by the harsh light and the disgust wrought there.

"That is rather the point," I said. "Given that rock troll society is led by those with the least amount of battle magic. You are fairly brimming over with it."

Eddie took another step backwards. Neja's knife flew through the air and whistled past him, landing with a *thok* in the wood of the dock. Eddie laughed. "You missed."

Neja said nothing, just glared. She also hadn't missed.

Her knife had cut right through the rope mooring the boat to the dock. With the strength of the current, the last few strands of rope holding the boat to the dock tore apart and the boat was free. It vanished out of view after only a few seconds.

Eddie realised this a moment too late, his hands barely touching rope before the boat disappeared. The song spell scroll slipped from his fingers and Tempest dived.

Two things then happened at once.

One: Tempest's talons closed around the scroll as she rescued it from the spray of the river. She turned towards me, the look on her face triumphant.

Two: Eddie lost his tenuous control on his battle magic and he shifted into a behemoth, his muscles like slabs, his limbs enough to crush a person. He roared, the sound reverberating through the entire mountain. I'd once seen Yolanda in her battle form, and she had been about twelve feet tall with a glare that could curdle milk. Eddie was so very much more than twelve feet tall, large enough that I would consider him a giant.

He reached out and batted Tempest from the air as she tried to wing her way to me. Her tiny form was no match for his magic-enhanced strength. The song spell scroll flew through the air, landing at Katrina's feet.

Tempest's wings crumpled and she hit the wall beside the door with a dull, terrible thud.

She did not move.

"Cal?" Yolanda was suddenly standing there in the door, looking at Tempest with wide eyes. Boulder was just behind her, chest heaving. They must have run after us, come to help us even though they should have been safe in their suites instead of here with Katrina and Neja and the two monsters who had lost control.

Because, even as I recognised Yolanda, recognised that she was my friend, there to help and there to keep this situation from getting any worse, I indeed lost control.

Eddie had hurt Tempest. Maybe killed her.

My pet.

My friend, even if only for a few days.

An innocent creature with such a joy for living.

Sebastian didn't rise up from within me like normal, turning the world into grey scale with halos of yellow around each living being whose life I could take. No, there was nothing so calm.

Sebastian—*I*—exploded outwards instead, intent on devouring all in my path.

CHAPTER 14

*P*erhaps the fracturing of my soul from the rest of me had hidden the true depths of what writhed beneath my skin, but what emerged when what little control I had snapped was worse than anything I could have imagined. The eldritch coils that twisted and turned were suddenly free, sinuous and shadowy, bound by four limbs that could tear and rend with claws sharp enough to gouge stone. My mouth was more muzzle and maw than organ for speech, the teeth meant to kill in a single touch. I could feel fire in my veins, not blood, and the sound that rumbled in my chest was as a growl was to a nuclear weapon. I was free, and the being who had made me cast off my chains was going to die.

The troll male, even for all his battle magic, could not possibly stand before me. He was so small, his life so insignificant before one such as me. I towered above him, my coils undulating, and felt joy at his horror. The sight of his pupils constricting into pinpoints with fear made me salivate. I could hear his heart beating so rapidly it might burst. The aura around him was a sickly yellow, so very close to death that I knew if I just breathed on him with intent, he would turn to dust.

In fact, *any* of the beings in the room would turn to dust if I so willed it. Even the djinn whose body was fuelled by smoke and magic rather than the blood of the trolls and the sand of the mountain nymph. They were all insignificant in comparison to what I was, to what power I had in the tip of my claw.

I was a Reaper of the sown. I was doom incarnate.

I watched as the troll male fell to his knees, jaw working silently as he tried and failed to form words. I lowered my head closer to his level, pressing my body against the stone of the floor. My proximity only seemed to exasperate matters; his battle magic fought helplessly against the thrall I had over him. In his desperation, he swung at me, the blow slipping through my shadowy coils as if they were fog.

I chuckled, the sound making the others behind me whimper.

"You think to *fight* me?" I asked. My voice was no longer the smooth, English voice that I had spoken with my entire life. Now, it purred with dark pleasure and held the tremors of ages untold. It was a voice that had not been heard on this plane of existence since the last Reapers walked free. I was the last, and would be sure not to be forgotten as they had been, cast to the ages. An instinctive part of me, somewhere in the part of my mind that was *other*, knew that my fellows had been lost, not forgotten, but the true meaning of those words was nothing to me. Not now, with my prey before me.

"P-please," the desperate troll whimpered. His battle magic was faltering, unable to stand up to me. In his true form he would be much weaker. I preferred some fight in my opponents, so I backed off a little. The battle magic stopped sparking, solidifying, though it did nothing to alleviate the fear-scent.

"Fool," I whispered, snaking my way through the dark shadows of the cavern. It was so easy to slip from one shadow to the next, as though they called to me, daring me to move between them, to explore the worlds that only the creatures born of shadows and stardust could know. I moved to the shadow by the door, wondering just how easy it would be to slip through that corridor and hunt other prey, prey that had the sense to scream rather than beg. Would I make the people pay for the mistake of their would-be king? I was just about to do so when my claws encountered something that was not shadow nor stone.

I hesitated.

Feathers. Fur. A tiny figure, limp and broken with not even a flicker of yellow to indicate that it lived. Something about the creature twisted whatever joy the hunt brought. I *knew* the creature, and I knew what had been done to it. Who had done this wretched thing.

I whirled back on the cowering troll. He had taken something glowing from the ground and was inching towards the river, as though that would bring him some escape. In his giant hand, swelled with magic, the glowing thing was only a twig, but it pulsated with power that was older than any in this cavern. The djinn might know its pull, but their ages smelled different. Similar, but not overlapping.

I lunged and snatched the thing from the troll's hand, my claws raking gouges in his skin. He let out a cry that rattled the pebbles on the bank of the river. I hissed at him for silence. He fell silent.

In my grasp, the thing was no more than an idea, too small to hold properly. It slipped through my claws and fell at the feet of the troll-who-was-not-a-troll. She picked it up and clutched it to her chest, looking at me with wide eyes. I lowered my head to stare at her and let out a growl. She trembled before me but did not cower, not as the male troll had done.

"Cal," she pleaded. As if that would mean anything to me.

I did not really care about the glowing thing after all, no matter it's untold power, for the scent of life recently snuffed from existence was still in the air. I had vengeance to exact for that toll, and no need for power, ageless or otherwise. I turned again to the male troll who was now on his knees, cradling his wounded hand against his chest. His battle magic had not withstood the touch of my claws and his form was once again small and trembling. Fine. This hunt was about retribution, not pleasure. No, that would have to wait.

"You," I said, twining about him with my coils, wondering just how far I'd have to squeeze to see him die. "Would you care to explain yourself before I kill you?"

The troll started sobbing, tears streaming down his

face, snot dripping from his nose and mixing with the blood on his hand. Pathetic. I exposed my fangs in disgust.

"I-I jus' wanted to be p-powerful," he hiccoughed. He could not even look at me as he spoke.

"Powerful?" I reared back my head, the thought of this weak, foolish creature before me aspiring to power. He was a mere speck of dirt to the reality of me. How could he possibly expect to be powerful? "Power has nothing to do with killing those who cannot defend themselves," I snarled, jerking my head to where the tiny body lay, beautiful and still.

The troll looked up at me, something in his eyes speaking not of desperation but of anger. Fury. Ah, yes, now we were getting somewhere interesting.

"I can't defend myself against you," he said, hunching his shoulders in a defeated pose. "If you're so *powerful*, you won't—"

"Kill you?" I laughed, loud enough to rattle stalactites from the ceiling. They splashed into the river, which devoured them whole. "Obviously you do not understand what I *am*."

I lay flat on the ground, my claws digging into the stone and leaving troughs in their wake. I looked the male troll, whimpering and smelling of terror, straight in the eye. "I am a Grim Reaper," I said, showing him my fangs. He recoiled. "I am the being in between Life and Death. I move in the shadows where light touches dark. I lead the hunt. I am the master of crossroads. I offer the choices to the choosers. And I defend the choiceless."

I lashed my tail out to sweep the limp body towards the troll, the feathers picking up the dirt of the cavern floor. Compared to the troll, the dead griffin was a songbird, barely large enough to see. I smoothed out the wings with a gentle claw so they lay flat against the body and curled the tail around the paws. Then, I pinned the troll in my gaze, pressing my will down upon him so that his back bent beneath my look and was made to see the destruction he had wrought.

"Do you think this one had a choice?" I asked. My voice was quiet enough that it did not echo in the darkness.

The troll sat up as best he was able, pressing against my will with whatever left remained of his own. "It was an animal. A pet. Nothing more. What does choice have to do with—"

I flattened the troll with my foot, my claws surrounding his body like a cage. The troll struggled for a few seconds, but the shadows I bore pressed closer and burned. He fell still.

A noise from behind me stopped me before I could kill my prey for his insolence. I snaked my head around to see who would prevent me from doing what needed to be done. The female troll, her hand clasped in the mountain nymph's, had taken a step forwards. She was trembling, too scared even to call on her own paltry battle magic. She swallowed, looked at the nymph, released his hand, and took another step forwards.

No, not scared, I realised with something akin to interest. Brave.

"You would protest what must be done?" I asked

her. She nodded once. "Why? What defence could you have for this creature?"

"Not for him," she said. The male troll pinned beneath my claws whimpered. She closed her eyes and took a breath. "Not for him. For you."

How intriguing. I studied her more closely. Her eyes were bright and wide but not afraid, though she stood before me in all my wrath. Her heart beat steadily, and though her hands were trembling, she did not cower or fight. The yellow aura around her was thrumming and bright, just a hint of shadows at the edges. She had a connection to Death. I could not harm her without first seeking his permission. Very well, it was not her I intended to kill. She was a curiosity, however. I brought my head closer to her.

"For me?" I asked, baring my teeth at her in a loose smile. I breathed shadows over her and she shivered. Her hands clenched at her side. She looked at me, meeting my gaze without hesitation.

"For you, Cal." Another step forwards. "Calvin Montgomery Thorpe, cousin to Baz, son to Teresa Thorpe, Knight of the Mortal Realms. Marketing agent for Death, errand boy for Life. Boss. Friend. Grumpy. An affinity for coffee that no one understands. An obsession with doing the right thing, just because it's right, even if the system doesn't say so. Soulless. Not heartless. A good human. A good *man*."

"Cal..." I rolled the word over my tongue. The same word that the troll-who-was-not-a-troll used. It was an interesting word, holding some familiarity. No, not familiarity, truth. It was a name. My name. It was who I was. If I wanted to, I could call the eldritch being whose skin I wore to heel and I would become myself again, glasses and all. My suit would probably be ruined, but I still had some pyjamas that were clean in my duffel bag.

I remembered who I was, now, and recognised just what was happening in this chamber. I knew that I held Eddie's fate in my hands and that the fear-scent coming from Katrina, Boulder, even Neja, was due to me. I was a living nightmare and my friends bore witness to the darkness.

I didn't call back Sebastian, though I could have done. I didn't hide from what I was. I just studied Yolanda, who had faced down the very darkest part of me so that I wouldn't do what I was about to do, so that I wouldn't stain my conscience, the one she believed was so good. Yes, I was all those things she described, but I was this, too. A Reaper. And I had a job to perform, no matter the consequences to myself.

Yolanda blinked at me, gave a wobbly smile, and nodded her understanding.

I turned back to Eddie, who was beginning to shiver as shock took hold of his system. He looked up at me. "Cal?" he asked hopefully.

"Yes," I said, my voice no longer wreathed in danger but still sharp.

"You don't have to do this," he said, holding out his hands in supplication. I saw the scratches there, knew that I had caused them, and did not regret it.

"I did not lie before," I said with a hiss. "When I told you what I am. You took the choice from one who could be nothing other than what she was. You manipulated your people into a path that would have inevitably led to a war they have been trying to avoid for generations, for more power than you already possess? You would tear the world of your people and all those who depend on you asunder for the sake of a single taste of the immortality of having your name spoken in legends. Your choices have led you here, to the crossroads. And it is now my job to give you one last choice."

I twisted closer, covering Eddie in my coils so that only he and I could hear the conversation that was to come. I could feel the others outside, desperate to push themselves in, smart enough to stay where they were.

"Just kill me!" Eddie snarled, a challenge.

"That is not your choice," I said, "for that is not my right. Your choice is either to return to the drome, to face the justice of your people for what you have done, or to leave. To never meet another of your kind for as long as you wander the world. To never draw upon your battle magic. To never again be a true rock troll. Accept your people, Eddie, or forsake them. That is the choice which I offer to you."

He may have been a weeping, sobbing mess only a few minutes before, but it was only now that I knew he was broken. I had done exactly what I needed to do, and I did not regret this any more than I regretted the scratches on his hand, but I did not take pleasure in it, either. I tightened my shadows around us, ready to bind him to whatever decision he made. Eddie just stared at me, blank, as if he couldn't contemplate what I had said.

I didn't know what justice his people would mete out, but if Yolanda's fate was anything of an indication, it would not let him live long. Perhaps long enough to ask forgiveness. Enough for that to matter.

Exile was what Katrina had described as Eddie's fate if he lost the trial pertaining to violating guestright. What I proposed was just more permanent, requiring his magic to be bound as well as to keep him away from his people, about whom he professed to care so much.

Eddie shuddered once and broke eye contact. "Let me leave," he said, voice barely audible. "I'll go away. Never come back. I promise."

"I'm afraid your promise means nothing to me. Though, I believe you that you will never come back, because my magic will bind you to your decision. Never again will you meet your people. Never again see their faces. Never again use your battle magic. Never ask for the forgiveness that I cannot grant, but your people can. Never see the future of your people. Never rejoice with them. Never mourn with them. You will be nothing to them, though they may ever live as nothing more than your fading memories. It is not the choice I would have made, but it was yours alone to choose. Edouard Rochefort, so are you bound."

Before he could do more than widen his eyes in understanding of what he had done, my shadows surged forwards and encompassed him, diving into him and wrapping themselves tightly around the core of his being. His battle magic fought me for a moment, futile though it was, then was surrounded and devoured by my shadows until there was nothing left. The shadows danced through his veins and back out through his skin, etching designs there in a language long dead that would bind their bearer forever. Eddie screamed.

He struggled for a few moments before falling still. His skin was now covered in a myriad of tattoos the exact colour of the shadows that lived inside and around me. The closer he got to his people, the darker they would become, inflicting pain until it became unbearable and he was forced to turn away.

I turned my back on Eddie and called Sebastian to order. As swiftly as the Reaper had exploded out of me, he folded back in. A moment later, I was standing on the bank of the river, my glasses still broken, my suit surprisingly intact if dusty. Tempest's body lay at my feet, her head turned towards me as if begging for the fish I promised her. She looked so peaceful.

I picked her up, cradling her body in my arms. "I'm sorry," I whispered into her feathers. "I'm so sorry."

A splash sounded behind me. I didn't turn around to witness Eddie swimming away, carried by the current of the river to some unknown clime. Instead, I looked towards the others, waiting near the door. Yolanda was exactly where I had left her, halfway to me, shoulders back, chin high, eyes shining as she looked on me with what I could only identify as pride.

"Come on, Cal," Yolanda said, holding out her hand

to me. I took it, cradling Tempest in my other arm. "Let's go get some popcorn."

"Popcorn sounds really good right now," I said. Yolanda squeezed my fingers. We went back to the passageway up to the world in companionable silence.

CHAPTER 15

$\mathcal{I}$f only everything were as simple as ending with a bowl of popcorn. Unfortunately, I had to answer for my actions—and explain Eddie's— before the tribe in the drome. We assembled just as before, only this time, I wasn't escorted to the drome by armed guards. I just filed in with everyone else, except I stood on the packed dirt and the others climbed into the stands.

Katrina, Yolanda, Boulder and Neja sat in the front row again, all watching me with nervous expressions. I'd like to say that our evening of relaxation and popcorn, with a few moments of me crying over the body of Tempest while Katrina took her away to be buried, put everything to rights, that all was as it was before, but that would be lying. Yolanda was still Yolanda. She and Boulder were ridiculously happy, twining their hands together as often as they could, speaking to one another in whispers surrounded by smiles. Anyone who looked at them could not possibly doubt the existence of soul mates.

But when they looked at me, there was a hesitation in their gaze, a hitch in their stride, a crack in their voices. Fear.

Katrina did not bother to hide her own fear, keeping a healthy distance from me while treating me with utmost respect. I think my genuine grief for Tempest made her warm up to me, but there was too much wariness to tell.

Neja, at least, did not show any outward signs of fear. She was dangerous enough to know her strength, and that she was far faster with a weapon than I could ever be. She knew that she was not in danger from me, not now and not ever if I could help it. But that intimacy we had shared in discussing my soul, the pieces of me that were fading away, that was gone. Instead, she was friendly. Just friendly.

It was an incredibly lonely thing, I realised, to be surrounded by people who would always keep their distance in one way or another. I wondered if this was how Death felt, despite knowing that everyone would come to him eventually. How Life was treated, despite being beloved by all. I didn't enjoy the feeling, but I didn't want anyone to be nice to me, override their fears and the pounding of their hearts, just because I was lonely in my power.

So I smiled at them as they watched me from the stands, ignored the weakness of their return smiles, and waited for the rest of the crowd to settle into place. The elders shuffled into their box and looked down at me. They didn't need to call for silence; no one was speaking. They just waited.

I was the only one left standing. I had faced their future king and he was gone under mysterious circumstances. The entire community had felt the tremors I had set off while fully inflamed in my Reaper abilities. They knew what I was and they knew that there was something terrible crawling beneath my skin, even if they hadn't witnessed it themselves. They, too, were afraid, but at least they didn't hide it.

"Reaper," the female elder said, looking down at me. "We hereby dismiss the questions regarding your guestright status. As your opponent has not deigned to appear here today, there can be no question as to your veracity."

I bowed my head in thanks. When I straightened my head, I was being pinned under the weight of her gaze. She took several breaths before speaking again, rallying her strength.

"However…" She sighed and looked over her shoulder at her companions. They nodded. The elder turned back to me. "However, we are informed by one Katrina Rochefort of what took place during the effort to retrieve the song spell scroll which belongs to our people and which Eduard stole. We are most grateful to you for helping to retrieve the scroll. But there is also the matter of your killing our future king."

I wasn't going to argue the future king point, despite the fact that my de facto winning of the trial meant Eddie couldn't possibly be king. There was no point in pouring salt on the wounds. No matter how much the rock trolls loved salt, there were lines I did not need to cross. Instead, I said, "He's not dead."

Gasps filled the air, swiftly followed by murmurs that were loud enough to drown out anything the elders might say. The trolls looked hopeful, but the dignitaries sent to watch the coronation just looked as though they were watching interesting television. Something that could never come true, but entertaining all the same. A fantasy. One brought about at the expense of the rock trolls.

The elders all beat their hands on their stone box, sending a *crack* reverberating through the drome. Silence fell, and the elder pointed her finger at Katrina. "Give your testimony!" she cried, almost apoplectic.

Katrina stood, her shoulders back and her chin high. "I was there, Reaper. Eddie died."

"He did not die," I said. "He went into the river to flee this place and the pain it caused him by being here. He is not dead; he will wander the world for the rest of his life, cut off from his battle magic and his people, but he is not dead."

You'd think I let Sebastian loose in front of the people by the way they stared at me in horror. Katrina sat abruptly, her mouth gaping. I explained what had happened before further demands could be made. I told them of my role in the world and the choice I had offered Eddie as punishment for taking the choice of another. I didn't give the details of how my magic bound him, or whether he knew the truth of what he was agreeing to, nor did I tell them how well and truly broken he had been at my offering. I told them only that I had offered him a choice, and he chose. I know that I didn't often display emotions properly, though my condition did appear to be improving, but the reaction to my simple explanation was really, really bad.

I shoved my hands into my pockets and tried not to feel the weight of everyone's stares on me. Sebastian writhed, turning its coils over and over, but I kept a tight hold on the urge to show my power, to prove to these people that I was a force to be reckoned with. In the stands, the trolls leaned on one another, some with tears in their eyes. The dignitaries, too, looked at me as if I had torn the ground from beneath them for banishing Eddie in so thorough a manner. A few, but only a very few, tried to hide their gleeful smiles as they watched the tragedy unfold around them.

"Cal," Katrina spoke, her voice soft and gentle and horrified. I looked at my friends to find Katrina and Yolanda looking at me as if I'd indeed personally killed their family member. Boulder looked alarmed but not upset. Neja's expression was hard, unreadable. "Cal," Katrina said again. "Do you understand what you've done?"

"Yes," I said. She shuddered. I turned back to the elders. "If I had returned Eddie here to face justice for violating guestright and stealing a sacred song spell, the cornerstone of your people's abilities here, you would have put him on trial and done what, had things gone as expected? Killed him, I would imagine, just as your former king threw his very own *daughter* off the side of a cliff for daring to love someone not of your tribe!"

The elder whipped her head to Yolanda. "Is this true?"

Yolanda stared straight ahead and said nothing, her hand clutched in Boulder's.

"Tell me that I am wrong, that Eddie's crimes against your people were not capital?" I snapped. I looked at any troll who would listen, settling on Yolanda. She closed her eyes and tried to fight a smile.

"It is true." The voice came from Mirabelle, and it was resigned. She stood there, gazing at her daughter and I knew she was answering more than my question. She had known about her daughter's fate, unlike the others it would seem, and still had been able to do nothing. She had to pretend that her daughter had abandoned them, just as the king had decreed. I understood, now, how cruel a thing that was, and not just to Yolanda. I still did not regret what I had done.

I kept talking, letting my friend have her few moments of peace, pretending that I didn't know what had just been revealed. "So he would have died if he'd been put on trial. And if he ran, he would have lived. That is what I offered him. I offered him the same choice you would have offered. Life, or Death. The choice I offered will be enforced, though. There is no return for Eddie, not here. He will remember his crimes his entire life. That was *his* choice."

"Very well, Reaper, we accept your actions," the elder said, though she would not look directly at me. "Now, if you will excuse us, we have a great deal to discuss, not the least of which is the line of succession."

"I do not understand," I said. "Your bloodline sits

right there. The second daughter of your former king. She should have been considered first, after Yolanda's leaving, should she not? Or have I misunderstood your rules?"

"She cannot—she is not even full-blooded troll!"

I scoffed and shook my head. This was so ridiculous, especially after everything else that had happened to me on this trip. "From what I understand, you choose your leaders based on the weakness of their battle magic, following a bloodline—not a marriage contract—until it dies out. Katrina Rochefort has the weakest battle magic of you all by simple virtue that she has none at all, being half-human. She is, however, well-versed in politics and economics and knows every one of your policies from the ground up. I would think that she would be an *ideal* candidate for your throne. However, if you need to search farther along the bloodline, I do not know what you will find. It is, though, none of my concern what you wish to do. I am not a member of your tribe."

I turned to leave when the elder shouted loud enough to draw me back. "Why would we take the second daughter when we have the first?"

I looked at Yolanda and tilted my head. She shook her head at me. I stepped towards her, stopping at the stone barrier between her and me. "It is your choice," I whispered, reaching for her. She took my hand with her free one and let out a choked sob.

"Please don't make me do this," she said. "I don't want to do this."

"Tell me what you do want," I said, squeezing her

fingers in rhythm, "and I'll do it. You're my friend, Yolanda. I owe you that and so much more."

She nodded and sniffled. Then, with more courage than anyone I'd ever seen, she told me what she wanted. I smiled. Boulder beamed. Katrina looked like she might cry with joy. Even Neja's expression softened. She looked at me and blinked in confusion before her expression hardened again. I pretended that I still felt nothing and ignored the ache that simple moment caused.

"Okay," I said, patting Yolanda's hand, "okay."

I walked back to the centre of the arena floor, looking up at the elders. "I am afraid that you cannot have her. Cast out by her father and abandoned by those she loves, she does not wish to come back. And what's more, she is marked by Death as one of his own. You cannot have her."

"She is ours!" the elder cried, slamming her fist on the stone.

"No," I said. "She is hers. And, in a moon's time, on the equinox, she will be Boulder's, as they join each other in marriage as mates. She has made her choice, and I, for one, will abide by it."

My earlier actions in the search of a choice must have been remembered, for I received no argument whatsoever. "When you have made your decision for the future of your people, please do let me know. I will give you my blessing and a gift. Though, you are not required to invite me again unless you truly wish to do so."

I turned again to leave and again was called back.

"Reaper."

I looked over my shoulder and found the female elder staring down at me with something firm in her gaze, tempered by what I thought might be sadness. I waited.

"You interfered in the ways of our people. Perhaps it turned out well this time, but do not expect it to be this way in the future. You are young. Untried. You have a great deal to learn." She pursed her lips, considering. "It has been a long time since the Reapers walked freely in Elsewhere. The immortals among us remember, but they are few, and relegated to their corners and dominions. The rest of us, well, we are not so used to being bound."

"I have no intention of binding you." And I didn't. I didn't want to get involved in these people's lives. I had enough to worry about. And yet, I knew that I was already neck deep in this. I had bound giants and angels to guard the mortal realms. I had travelled through Faerie and got directly involved in stopping a war between the Courts. What I really needed was to learn more about the Reapers, and I couldn't do that if I faded away.

I was beginning to feel pulled in too many directions.

"Intentions and actions are two very different things," the elder said. She sighed and waved her hand. "Go. Leave us be. We will decide things without you."

I nodded, bowed, and turned to leave. To my surprise, Yolanda and Boulder came with me. Neja, too, jumped over the stone barrier from the arena and jogged to catch up with me. She slipped her arm through mine.

"We all make mistakes, Cal," she whispered.

I shivered as we transitioned from the bright outdoors to the interior of the cavern. It might have been well-heated but it was close and dark, too.

"You think I made a mistake?" I asked. My voice had no inflection to it because I didn't know whether I was asking or accusing.

"Giving in to your powers, binding Eddie like that… it was a little overhanded, don't you think?" Neja shrugged. "I know a little bit about mistakes. People use my wish magic desperately and rarely know the true consequences until it's too late."

I could attest to that. Al Capone had suffered for it. As had I.

"Maybe it was a mistake," I murmured.

"No." Yolanda said. I turned to face her. She still stood tall, her pride unbowed by the last few days, no matter that I had done almost nothing to fulfil my promise. I hadn't made her people see how awesome she was, I'd just made them realise their desperation. But there she was, in jeans and a t-shirt, looking fiercer than any warrior I'd met. Her fingers were twined with Boulder's and her shoulders were back, her chin high. "It was not a mistake."

"Surely you can't—" Neja protested.

"Cal defended a being who could not defend itself," Yolanda said, glaring at Neja. "He saved my people from ruin and war under a leader that cared more for ambition than our culture and ways. He is a good person!"

Neja studied Yolanda for a moment, her arm still twined in mine. Then, she looked at me. She reached up and straightened my broken glasses. "Okay," she whispered. "I see."

I gave her my best smile, but it must have been a little lopsided because everyone burst out laughing. I sighed and shrugged.

"So," I said. "Do we have to travel back by that weird rock shifting technique or is there a less terrifying way of getting back to Death's lands? Because, frankly, I'd like to avoid the sensation of being crushed by rocks if I could. Given the week I've had and everything."

Yolanda's grin was wide and very visibly mocking my despair. I grumbled and told her that she was responsible for my dry-cleaning bill.

CHAPTER 16

eath was generally very polite, unlike Life, unless he was dealing with my mother, in which case he became frustrated and ignored such things as common courtesy. This time, he wasn't dealing with my mother. Instead of bursting in on my flat, he knocked gently and waited until I opened my door. Then, he stepped into my living space without so much as a by-your-leave.

"I think some tea would be nice. Do you have the proper equipment, or are you equipped only to make coffee?" he asked, moving towards my kitchen.

"Why, hello," I said to the empty hallway. "Please come in. I have all the drink making accoutrements, would you like something?"

"Where do you keep your mugs?" Death called from the kitchen. I closed the door and tried not to grumble as I shuffled my way back to the kitchen and started the process of making tea.

"Is there a particular reason why you're stopping by

today, or did you forget to stock your own kitchen? Not that I don't mind sparing a cup of tea—or coffee—but you usually have a reason for barging into my flat without warning." I leaned against the counter and folded my arms while waiting for the kettle to boil. Death splayed his hands on the granite and studied me. It was always unsettling to be the focus of those terrible voids that were his eyes, but this time, Sebastian reared up and hissed.

"I thought as much," Death murmured. He gestured to the table. "Sit down, Cal. We need to have a talk."

I did as directed, as stunned by Sebastian's adverse reaction to Death's scrutiny as I was by Death's sense of concern. Nothing concerned Death. Not that I had seen. Not like this. Death poured out the tea and set a cup in front of me, already sweetened. I sipped at the liquid and winced. Tea was all well and good, but coffee was much preferred. Especially if Death was going to be the bearer of bad news.

Death sat across from me and took his time doctoring his own tea. After stirring the liquid several times, he spoke. "I take it that the week in the domain of the rock trolls was not uneventful?"

"Not particularly," I said. "Did Yolanda tell you what happened?"

"Some, though the djinn Neja mentioned something in passing when she departed yesterday. I had surmised enough on my own, however, to not require their veiled statements. I am not unaware of the ripples in the balance, and know when certain forces are… active." Death stared at me again and Sebastian writhed in obvious discomfort. I added another spoonful of sugar to my tea; I was going to need the extra sweetness to get through this conversation.

"Eddie, the heir to the throne, fled with the trolls' song spell scroll and I followed with the miniature griffin Tempest leading the way. She'd taken a liking to me, I guess, and was given to me as a gift." I cupped my hands around the cup of tea, staring into its depths. I didn't think I could face looking at Death for this conversation. "Eddie killed her and I…"

"Reacted?" Death asked.

"That is one way of putting it." I shook my head. "I thought that my Reaper abilities were just what they had always done before: turning the world black and white except for those halos of yellow telling me how close people are to dying. And if I touch them, then I kill them, drawing their lifeforce into myself. But this… it was a creature, a monster of shadows. I wasn't myself when I was this thing, but I knew who I was. I also knew other things that I couldn't possibly have known. I asked Yolanda if she would sketch what I really looked like and she turned nearly white at the thought. Neja wouldn't even consider it."

I chanced a look at Death. He was sitting there, as immaculate as ever in his three-piece suit, his purple pocket square the only splash of colour. His skin seemed to suck in the light and the shadows that constantly writhed around him seemed to dance over my skin as well. I pulled back, setting my hands in my lap.

"The Grim Reapers can access their abilities by

varying degrees, depending on the severity of the situation. They manifest, though, as their own nightmares. You manifested, Cal. It's not something to be treated lightly. It usually only happens a few times in a Reaper's existence, when they must perform a task that would otherwise be beyond them, or when they are severely injured, or when they are dying."

My breath hitched. "I thought Reapers were immortal," I breathed.

"They are. But everything dies, Cal. Even immortals." Death made a sympathetic sound. "It is rare, but it happens."

I swallowed. My mouth was suddenly dry. Somehow, I didn't think I could swallow another mouthful of tea if I tried. I pushed the cup away. "I had to…be killed to prove that Eddie violated guestright. Neja did it, a knife to the eye. It should have been simple enough. I've had this happen before, and it always hurts, but the pain goes away. This time, while I was dead, I saw Sebastian."

"Sebastian?" Death cocked his head.

"It's what I call my Reaper abilities." I rubbed my neck. "It was me, but not. And he said that I was fading, because my soul was missing and we weren't meant to be a Reaper without the soul to bind the abilities and myself together."

Death hummed, the sound thoughtful but unhelpful. "How far had the fading progressed?"

I wiggled the fingers on my left hand.

"I see."

We sat in silence for a moment. I would like to say

that sitting and having a cup of tea with my boss was a pleasant experience, but at that moment I wanted to be almost anywhere else, doing almost anything else. I wanted to be ignorant and grumpy again. I didn't want to be afraid.

But I was.

"I cannot prevent the fading. It will progress, and I cannot predict how quickly. Months, a year, less…it depends on a great number of factors. The fact that you manifested could have been due to Eddie's battle magic, if he was as strong as Yolanda suggests, or it could be that—"

"I'm dying," I croaked. I lay my head on the table and thought hard about pushing down my panic. Then, I realised that I wasn't panicking and I sat up again. I was calm. I was unsurprised by Death's statement and I was not freaked out. But I was definitely afraid.

"If you find your soul, then it can be put to rights, but otherwise, yes. You are dying." Death finished his cup of tea. I thought about asking if he wanted more, but found I was unable to do so. I was unable to do much of anything just then.

"How do I find my soul?" I finally managed to ask. I searched his face in desperation. "Have you had any new information on its whereabouts?"

Death spread his hands in supplication. "I still cannot find your soul. Life, too, has been similarly unable to discern its whereabouts, which has frustrated her quite a bit. Despite her, ah, bluster, she is rather fond of you, Cal. As am I."

"Do you know, that doesn't actually make me feel better."

Death chuckled. "It doesn't surprise me. What of your djinn? Has she discovered anything?"

I winced. Neja had found a note from Croatia some seven hundred years old that had been written in my handwriting, signed with my signature, that I didn't write. It could only have been from my soul, but it only provided more questions than answers. As frustrating as it was, I studied it more than I cared to admit. It was in my pocket almost all the time, a constant reminder of everything I'd lost. I pulled it out and handed it to Death.

"'The employment was a mistake.' What is this?" He turned the note over and frowned. "You signed this?"

"No," I said. "We think my soul did."

Death set the note down gently. "I see."

"Do you know what it means?" I asked. If he didn't know, then I was well and truly lost and without hope.

"I…might," Death said, drawing out the last word. He shook his head. "It's not something I care to discuss at this moment. Nor do I think it's relevant to the location of your soul. The note, how old is it?"

"Seven hundred years or so. Why?"

"When you travelled back in Time, you only went to 1494, correct?"

I nodded. Did some math. Then, "Oh. My soul didn't end up in the same time as I did when it got lost. It hasn't been travelling linearly."

Death nodded. "I'm afraid not. It likely jumped

around, stopping in places that called to it. Souls can be tricky like that."

It figured that my soul would be one of the tricky ones. "So how do we actually find it? Talk to Time?"

"No," Death said emphatically. "Time has enough problems of his own at the moment. I told him he shouldn't get involved with that agency of his, but he never listens. No. Time will be of no help."

"If you don't know, and Life doesn't know, and Time can't help, then what?" I snapped. Desperation was beginning to sound like hopelessness and I didn't much care for that.

Death leaned back in his chair and steepled his fingers, resting his hands on the table. "There are stories as old as the Elderkin—the old gods—about those who weave the tapestries of the world, seeing to the individual threads that make up the larger picture. It is possible—mind you, possible is not a certainty— that you may find the path to your soul talking to one of these beings."

"What like the Greek Fates?" I vaguely remembered stories about those beings who held the threads of life in their hands and cut them when a person was meant to die. Since I hadn't seen any threads in Life's hands or house, I had a feeling it was only somewhat accurate.

Death nodded, rubbing the back of the neck. "They are…similar, yes. Many of the names for such beings— being, really, since the others are projections of the first—have long been forgotten. But they still exist. They have not faded away, like many other Elderkins have done."

"The Morrigan was an Elderkin," I said, remembering the goddess who had interfered in the situation with the Fae, manipulating me the whole time. I hadn't much taken to such manipulation, or her.

"The Iron Witch, too," Death said, bringing up another "opponent" of mine who had spilled my cup of coffee. I had been trapped in a binding circle with her, the first realisation that I was more than human, though human I still remained. I know, I know, my life doesn't much make sense sometimes.

"So, what, I have to go back to the Goblin Market?" I asked. The market was a place of magic so strong that it permeated the air. The buildings moved, the creatures there were many and they had really good food stalls.

Death sighed. He leaned forwards until he was resting his elbows on the table. He dipped a finger in his tea and let three droplets fall onto the table. "The being to whom I refer is older than many Elderkin. She will not be so easily found at the Goblin Market, though it is a good place to start. I can give you a token that will guide you to her. I warn you, Cal, it will not be a safe journey, even for one such as yourself. Dying—many times over—is the least of your problems."

"Do…" I broke off, not sure how to proceed, not sure I wanted to. I swallowed what little pride I still possessed and spoke again. "Do I have to go alone?"

"Yolanda will not be able to accompany you. She has not the mettle," Death answered. I shook my head, staring at the droplets on the table. They sat there, slowly shrinking as the heating in my kitchen dried the air. I could have sworn that if I looked closely enough, then I would see images in those droplets, perhaps of things that would matter greatly to me. I didn't look.

"Yolanda is busy with Boulder. They've moved in together. They're getting married in a month," I said. I smiled faintly. "I'm happy for her."

Death cocked his head, studying me intently. "Truly?"

I nodded.

"Your emotions are stronger than before."

"Is that a good thing or a bad thing?" His voice was telling me it was a bad thing, but his expression was unreadable, which could have meant anything from he was intrigued to he was absolutely confused.

He shook his head. "I do not know. Your condition is unique, and it is dangerous. I would advise you to go on this quest as quickly as possible. Your soul *must* be found. An empty Reaper is one I will have to dispose of. Permanently."

I winced.

"I am curious, though. If you did not intend to take Yolanda with you, then who—oh, of course. Your djinn friend." Death leaned back in his chair. He nodded. "Indeed. Yes. I believe that she could survive the journey, being what she is. It will not be an easy thing for her, and I think that both of you will come out changed, but if she wishes to accompany you, then she may."

I nodded. Good. Of course, I'd have to actually ask Neja to go on this highly perilous journey to a being older than the forgotten gods so I could find some direction to my soul. Maybe I could bribe her with cookies or dinner.

"Okay," I said, my voice more of a croak than anything. I cleared my throat, finished my cup of tea without gagging, and sat up straight. "Okay. What sort of token do I need?"

Death unbuttoned his suit jacket, then his waist-coat, then his shirt, which was a little unusual given that he'd never been anything but immaculate and fully dressed. Thankfully—for both my sanity and my sense of propriety—Death stopped there. He reached in towards his chest, hand writhing with shadows, and for a moment I thought he was going to grab an amulet or something. Then, his shadows pierced his skin.

The world screamed, a high pitched sound that made me cower and cover my ears, eyes squeezed shut. The sound stopped a moment later. I waited several beats, just to be sure, then opened my eyes. Death sat there, as before, no wound to be seen. Impossible, though, because in his hand, as dark as the shadows that lived in his skin and the void between the stars, was his heart. Still beating.

My jaw worked open and closed a few times. I squeaked, about all the speech I could manage. I looked at him desperately.

"Yes, it is my heart," Death said. "And a jar to put it in would do nicely."

I mechanically rose and fetched a jar, holding it out and watching with fascinated horror while Death deposited the organ into the jar. He closed the lid and pushed the jar across the table towards me. I nodded, tucking my hands into my lap. I didn't really want to touch it, even encased in glass.

"My heart will lead you to the being you need to find. Be careful with it. It is immensely powerful and will call to any number of creatures craving that power. Your own abilities will mask much of my aura, but not all."

"Right," I said weakly. "So, um, does this being I need to find have a name?"

Death smiled, the motion cracking whatever sanity I had left. I whimpered.

"Indeed, though I usually just call her Mother."

Oh, great. As if this day weren't bad enough.

—

The End.

ACKNOWLEDGMENTS

Thank you to all the readers out there who have come this far with me and Cal. (Poor Cal.) You mean so very much to me and I cannot possibly thank you enough.

Thanks also to my amazing cover designer, Fay Lane, who has done the covers for this series as well as several other of my books. Her designs are an inspiration for me to keep writing this series, and also to create many more just to have something worth her covers.

Special thanks to those who have been with me from the beginning, listening to my ranting on various ways to torture—I mean, develop—Cal and make this series more interesting. I could not have done it without you.

ABOUT THE AUTHOR

E.G. Stone is an independent author who has been writing, creating and causing vast amounts of trouble since the age of six. Since then, E.G. has improved rather a lot in both the trouble-causing and writing and now spends her time writing fantasy and science fiction. When not writing, she is off musing about the workings of languages, both real and created, or drawing and sewing. E.G. reads voraciously, perhaps to the point of slight-insanity. Weird, nerdy, perhaps a little crazy, she is having a grand old time writing, reading, reviewing, interviewing, and, naturally, continuing her endeavours in causing trouble.

www.ingramcontent.com/pod-product-compliance
Lightning Source LLC
Chambersburg PA
CBHW031011190726
48286CB00003BA/795